"This must be Babe.

Emma's attention was torn. "Babe, stay back. Don't come off the porch."

Josiah took advantage of her attention moving away from him and stepped several feet closer.

"Stop! Both of you." Emma turned her focus back to Josiah even as she heard Babe's dainty footsteps bouncing down the stairs. Neither person listened to her admonition to stop.

"Hello, sweetheart." Josiah greeted Babe with a soft voice. His entire countenance changed, as if he were viewing an angel in the flesh.

"Hello, Papa," Babe responded, racing past Emma before she could stop her.

Emma watched in disbelief as her daughter flew into the surprised man's arms. The little girl buried her face in his shoulder before peeking up at her mother. "See? I told you God would send my papa to our doorstep."

PAIGE WINSHIP DOOLY enjoys living in the warm panhandle of Florida with her family, after having grown up in the sometimes extremely cold Midwest. She is happily married to her high school sweetheart, Troy, and they have six homeschooled children. Their oldest son, Josh, now lives in Colorado, while the newest blessing, Jetty, rounds out the family in a wonderful way. The whole family is active in Village Baptist Church. Paige has always loved to write. She feels her love of writing is a blessing from God, and she hopes readers will walk away with a spiritual impact on their lives and smiles on their faces.

Books by Paige Winship Dooly

HEARTSONG PRESENTS
HP84—Heart's Desire

Treasure in the Hills

Paige Winship Dooly

Heartsong Presents

To my family: You are all so precious to me! Thank you for the support and the blessings and joy you've brought into my life. I love you all and am so proud of each of you. Thanks also to my husband, Troy, my mother, Sharon, and my good friend Rhonda for your critiques of this story.

A note from the Author:
I love to hear from my readers! You may correspond with me by writing:

Paige Winship Dooly
Author Relations
PO Box 721
Uhrichsville, OH 44683

ISBN 978-1-59789-656-6

TREASURE IN THE HILLS

Our mission is to publish and distribute inspirational products offering exceptional value and biblical encouragement to the masses.

PRINTED IN THE U.S.A.

one

Deadwood, Dakota Territory, 1876

Babe's incessant chatter would be enough to send old Ben Parson into an early grave. The dignified man seemed to enjoy the entertainment, but he probably needed a break. His white hair stood on end where he'd run wet hands through it a few too many times, but his crinkle lines of laughter were at full depth as he listened to Babe talk. He did appear to enjoy the little girl's stories.

Emma Delaney sat back on her heels and watched as her five-year-old daughter took a quick breath before resuming her continuous speech. Too far away to hear what the tiny blond spoke of, Emma knew it would have something to do with her imaginary life and pretend friends. Babe lived in a fantasy world almost as much as she lived in reality. Emma decided now might be a good time to back off on the fairy tales they'd been reading.

"Don't you be bothering Mr. Parson too much, Babe. Come on over by me and give the man a moment of peace." Emma put a hand to her forehead to shade her eyes and watched for her precocious daughter to do as she'd bidden.

"But Ma, I'm in the middle of a story! I can't stop right here and leave Mr. Parson wondering what's gonna happen next!" Babe looked aghast over the thought that her captive audience would be left hanging. "Can I have a few more minutes, please?"

"She ain't a bother to me, Mrs. Delaney. The day passes a mite bit faster for me with her and her stories." Ben shifted his stiff body but didn't miss a beat of working his gold pan. "It'll be a sad day when this girl grows up and I won't have her by my side. She keeps my mind young."

Emma felt a pang of regret. "If you're sure. But you send her on over this way if your mind needs a break."

"Will do." Ben nodded at Babe to continue, and the sound of her sweet childish voice resumed. It carried along the stream before disappearing into the trees.

If only Ben knew that his dreaded day already hovers at his doorstep.

Emma pushed the melancholy thought aside and shrugged her shoulders, trying to ease the tautness that built up in them throughout the day. No matter how many breaks she took, the tension always remained and pulled her muscles tight as if they were hooked to a pulley. If she continued to pan for gold as she did now, her shoulders would be so tight they'd hitch up and settle permanently somewhere near her ears. Her body told her to hand over the claim to Mack and move on.

She'd realized of late that the fog of grief caused by the death of her husband, Matthew, two years earlier had lifted, and she felt ready to live again. In the time in between, she'd done well to lift one foot and put it in front of the other. The days had passed in a blur. She didn't know when things had changed—or when she'd begun to see the world more brightly again—but they had.

Her rediscovered joy in her young daughter led to a

deeply buried desire to spend longer periods of time with her. Babe, no longer the complacent toddler who stayed at her feet, now wandered off farther and farther, and the day would come when Emma looked up from her work to find that her little girl had disappeared. It wasn't safe to have her around the stream and woods with little supervision.

The miners Emma worked near were safe, watching over both females and stepping in the few times someone got out of line, but others weren't so trustworthy. Most of the men at the stream had rented sleeping space in the Delaneys' barn and continued to do so, an arrangement that had allowed her to feel safe enough to continue work on the claim after Matthew had passed away. Already familiar with the boarders, she felt it prudent to keep the arrangement for her and Babe's security and protection.

One particular miner, Mack, had gone so far as to insist she hand the running of her claim over to him. He assured her that any find would profit her first and that he'd take nothing more than a small share to provide for his own needs. Emma knew she wanted to keep Matthew's dream alive and that work was the best thing to prevent her from breaking down from the devastation after her loss. But it was time for a change.

"Mama!" Babe's excited voice announced her arrival moments before she appeared. "We found gold! Mr. Ben said I could keep it! See?"

The tiny girl thrust the miniscule nugget in front of Emma's eyes, nearly blinding her in the process.

Emma laughed as she pushed the small hand a bit farther back from her face. "I won't see if you poke me in the eye with it. Let me take a peek."

The "nugget," not much more than a grain of dust in Emma's opinion, lay treasured in the palm of Babe's sweaty hand. "Oh, it's beautiful, baby! Shall we place it with the others in our bag?"

Babe nodded, and Emma pulled the small fabric bag from a hidden pocket of her dress. The worn bag matched everything else they owned, but it served its purpose. The tiny weave of the fabric kept even the smallest of nuggets safe. "That's a pretty special find. If it were any bigger, I'd have to insist that Mr. Parson keep it for himself."

"Oh, he's found plenty bigger than this! He said he's having a right good day today, and this one's my reward for keeping him okipied."

"Occupied," Emma corrected. "You're a good girl to keep him company. Run and tell him thanks for the nugget and tell him we'll see him in the morning."

Babe ran off to do as she was told. Emma took advantage of the last few moments of quiet to gather up her supplies and wash up a bit. She wished she'd had what she could call a good day. The few dusty nuggets in her bag wouldn't add up to any value. But she plodded along because she knew they showed there was more than met the eye, if only she could find the treasure that evaded her. In time, the tiny finds would grow to be enough.

The family had moved to the outskirts of Deadwood when the rush first started and had a choice claim in the hills. Matthew had worked long days, and Emma accompanied him on most of them. As long as infant Babe stayed in a good mood, Emma worked right alongside her husband. Their cabin, rustic but secure, didn't take much maintenance, and Emma realized early on that she grew bored without a purpose to occupy her mind. She couldn't think of anything better than to be at the side of the man she loved, her best friend, as they worked to reach their dream.

Babe trotted over, and Emma rose stiffly to her feet. "Your mama's poor old body can't take this much longer, baby girl."

"You're not as old as Mr. Parson, Mama, and I'm *not* a baby girl!" A huff accompanied the statement.

"I stand corrected." Emma ruffled her daughter's unruly hair. The tidy braids that had been in place early that morning when they left their house were now more fluffs of curl than anything else. She plucked a leaf from the top of Babe's head. "Did you tell your stories while balanced on your head today?"

"Of course not!" Babe giggled. "But I did do some rolls down the hill by the fallen tree. Head over heel, all the way down to the stream. At the bottom I crashed into Mr. Duggin and knocked him into the water. But he wasn't mad. He said he needed to cool off anyway."

Oh my. Nothing but a lady, my daughter. Emma hid a grin. She'd make a stop by Phil Duggin's claim to apologize. Anyone else and she'd be mortified, but Phil was a trickster and would take the unexpected bath in stride. Men all along the stream whiled away the hours planning their strategies to get even with Phil's continuous pranks.

They began the trek home, and she glanced over at her daughter as she skipped along at Emma's side. Maybe it was time to switch the little girl over to pants like the men and boys wore. At least her pantaloons wouldn't be flashing as she raced down the hill. Emma knew the other miners loved Babe's childish antics, but she didn't need to put on a show. Or maybe it was confirmation that their time on the hill had come to its end, confirmation that Babe would wander and get into danger or situations that weren't best for a five-year-old. "Well, I think from the looks of your hair you brought part of that hill back with you."

She slowed her steps to match her daughter's and weighed her next words. "Babe, what would you think about spending our days at the cabin instead of up here on the hill?"

Babe's face, full of trust, tilted up so she could peer at Emma's. "Like on the Sabbath?"

"Like on the Sabbath, yes, but every day in between, too."

"I think that would not be fun. I like coming up to the hills. Jimmy Jacobs says he hates being home all the time with his ma. He says I'm lucky we get to go to the claims every day like his pa. His big brothers get to go, but he has to stay home. I don't want to be mad like Jimmy Jacobs while you go to the hills without me."

"I'd be at the cabin with you, sweetheart. I didn't mean I'd leave you behind." Emma suppressed her smile. Jimmy, Babe's closest friend, always longed to be like his older brothers. She didn't realize the five-year-old boy talked so much with her daughter. Where were the days when the two had sat on a blanket on the floor and screamed over a mutually desired block or spoon at Emma's and Katie's feet?

"Oh, that's different. . .a little bit. But what would we do all day?"

"We can explore around our house, so you'd still be in the hills every day. And we can start your lessons. I think you're more than ready. We can sew some pretty dresses.

You grow like a weed, and I can barely button the tops of your bodices around you." She quieted as they reached Phil's claim. "Good evening, Mr. Duggin. I understand my daughter caused you some excitement this afternoon."

"Hello, Mrs. Delaney." Phil Duggin jumped to his feet, pulled his cap off, and worried it with his hands. His already ruddy face burned bright red. "It was nothing, ma'am, just a child having fun. I think we all know it's high time a prank turned my way."

"Long past due," a male voice called from downstream.

Phil ignored him. "If anyone were to get me, I'd love for it to be your daughter every time. That child can put a smile on the surliest man's face."

Another voice called their way through the twilight: "But we *will* get you, Duggin. When you least expect it." Laughter drifted up and down the stream. Phil had a lot of buddies who were anxious for their moments to get back at him. All in the name of friendship.

Phil flashed Emma a smile. "Anything to pass the time, ya know?"

"I do," she agreed. The days grew long, especially in the rougher weather. "Well, we'll be on our way, then. I wanted to make sure you were well after your tumble."

"I'm no worse for wear. You all have a good evening, now."

"We sure will. Thank you for your patience with my daughter."

They continued on, and Mack stood as they neared his partner's claim. "Hold on a minute and I'll walk you home."

She watched him as he worked. A man who took pride in his appearance, he had nondescript brown hair, long though trimmed, and pale blue eyes that were constantly watching her. The notion unnerved her at times, but she knew he felt it his duty to watch out for them now that Matthew was gone. Mack didn't like Emma and Babe to walk the short distance home alone, and he never failed to remind her. Emma knew her chance to discuss Mack's work with the claim had come.

"I'm all packed up and ready to go. Let's hit the trail." He ruffled Babe's hair, but she ignored him.

Emma found it odd that Babe warmed up to every other man on the mountain, but Mack, sweet as he could be, couldn't break through the icy shell that encased her daughter when he came around. She glanced over to see how he took the latest rejection. He didn't seem bothered in the least.

"Mack. . ." Now that the time had come, the words stuck in her throat. She cleared it and tried again. It was best to get it over with. "Mack, I think it's time for me to hand over the reins of the claim to you. That is, if you're still interested."

Mack's eyes lit up. "Are you serious? I've waited a long time for you to make that decision. About two years, as a matter of fact. You and the baby need to be at home, not working up here on a dirty claim."

"I'm not a baby! Don't call me that. My name is Babe." Babe stared up at him, hands clenched into fists at her sides.

Emma jumped at the vehemence in Babe's voice. She knew she'd made the right decision. Her daughter needed more of her time and training. No longer would the small child be allowed to run wild to intermingle with the ruffians who worked the mountain. She dropped to her knee and took Babe by the arms. "Babe, you apologize to Mr. Mack at once. You know better than to talk to adults that way."

Babe sent her a glare before turning to face Mack. "I'm *sorry,* Mr. Mack, but in the future you may now only call me Miss Delaney."

Emma gasped at Babe's outright defiance. Where had her sweet little girl gone? Had she waited too long to leave the claim? She needed to talk to Katie Jacobs.

"Mack, I don't know what's gotten into Babe, but I need to deal with her alone. If you don't mind, I'm going to stop off at Katie's before we head for home."

Mack's reluctance showed. "I don't like you walking alone, even for this short distance." They'd reached the clearing around her friends' place.

"I'll make sure one of Katie's boys accompanies us the rest of the way to the cabin. We'll be fine."

"If you're sure. I looked forward to the rest of the walk so we could discuss how to handle the change of hands with the claim. When do you want me to start? Tomorrow?"

"I hadn't thought that through. I've only just made the decision." She paused for a moment. "How about I finish out the week, and then we can start fresh with the changes on Monday. I need to prepare the men around us. Losing Babe's company will hit hard for some of them." She glanced over at her sober daughter. "But we can visit. We'll make sure to stop by often."

"That will be good. I need to make arrangements with my partner for the other claim, too."

Mack peered at Babe, and Emma couldn't discern his expression. Exasperation? Disappointment? No, it was a look of anger and resentment. She knew her daughter had been rude, but as an adult, Mack should know that children weren't always the most angelic beings. For that matter, most adults didn't know to hold their tongues when they should. She didn't want to excuse Babe's poor behavior, but Mack's facial expression took her by surprise.

She herded Babe ahead of her down the path that led to the Jacobses'. Mack didn't hide his intentions to court Emma, but so far Emma wasn't at a place where she could face a future with another man. She might be coming out of her haze of grief, but that was a far cry from wanting another man in her life.

If she were honest with herself, she knew deep down inside she had her own reservations about Mack. Something held her back, but she couldn't put her finger on what it was. She felt secure with him running her claim, but for now that was the extent of her trust. His response moments earlier had only increased that catch in her spirit. A shiver of apprehension passed through her.

two

Katie, a strikingly beautiful woman even as she headed into middle age, stood in her yard and gathered laundry from the lines her husband had hung for her. Emma felt a pang of longing. An identical set hung in her yard, placed there by Matthew. Would the reminders never quit? Maybe she should consider moving on, away from the place where her memories lingered. If she were to make a change, why not change everything? She and Babe could move to a real city and get far away from Deadwood.

She shuddered at the thought. No way. She wasn't that far along yet. She couldn't leave and give up all she'd shared with her husband. Letting loose of the claim would be enough for now. She'd take one day at a time and figure out her future later.

"Do my eyes deceive me, or did my good friend Emma Delaney finally show up for a visit?" Katie called out. She stood with her hand shading her eyes. Her black hair was upswept, and she looked cool and fresh, even in the late afternoon heat.

Emma felt like a clod next to her. She swept back the blond strands of hair that had escaped the twist at the back of her neck to hang in front of her face. She knew her own brown eyes were etched with exhaustion. "Are we intruding? If so, we can come back on a different day." Emma now questioned her decision to stop by Katie's. The

15

men would be home soon, and Katie had to be knee-deep in dinner preparations. She followed her friend onto the front porch.

"You know you never intrude when you visit. C'mon in here and get off your feet." They entered the cabin. "I'll get you something cool to drink. Babe, Jimmy's out in the barn. Why don't you go tell him you're here?" Katie bustled around the room while Babe scurried off to find Jimmy.

Emma watched out the window to make sure her daughter arrived at the rugged building in one piece. "Can I help? I've been sitting all day."

"No, you relax, and I'll sit with you in a moment."

Emma grabbed up some towels and bedding from the basket Katie had set beside the table. She began to fold while Katie threw a snack together. "Will the men be home soon? I don't want to interfere with your dinner."

Katie waved her words away. "They plan to work as late as daylight will allow. The days are growing shorter, and Hank's worried that we don't have much time left before winter hits with all its fury." She pointed a thin finger toward the wood-framed fireplace, where a kettle hung over kindling that crackled and popped with heat. "I have stew in the pot ready to go when they walk through the door. I can visit. What's on your mind?"

"I'm about to make some changes, and I need your encouragement. . .and prayers. I really need your prayers more than anything." Emma continued to fold as she spoke. "I'm going to leave the claim. Mack will take over, and I know it's silly, but I feel like I'd be a disappointment to Matthew. But I have to think of Babe, and she's starting to wander and her attitude is changing. I feel she needs more of my time and attention."

"First of all, you know you always have my prayers, even when we go weeks without seeing each other. You're on my list every day."

Emma felt some of the pressure let up at her friend's sweet words. Of course Katie prayed for them. She always had. Emma knew that.

"Second of all, I doubt Matthew would have expected you to keep up the claim in the first place, so you sure aren't failing him now. I think it's a great idea to let Mack take over. He's cared for you for a long time, and I'm sure he has your best interests at heart. In my busybody opinion, you need to take that next step."

Emma glanced up. "And that step would be?"

Katie leaned forward and took Emma's hand in hers. "Darling, you've been alone a long while now. It's time you found a man for yourself, and a pa for Babe. We worry about your being alone all the time way out here. Mack seems like a nice enough man. Maybe you should give him a chance, show him some interest."

Emma jerked her hand away and stood to pace across the floor. "I'm not at that place yet. I'm getting there, Katie, and I appreciate your concern, but I'm not ready." Her gaze took in the large room.

A sheet separated the sleeping quarters from the cooking area. Katie had her treasured rocking chair that Hank had crafted for her pulled up near the fire. Though sparse, the room felt warm through Katie's creative use of fabric and flowers. Little treasures and collectibles that she'd accumulated through the years sat on small shelves that

Hank had placed on the various walls. Emma knew there was a doorway on the sleeping side that led to a newer room Hank had built on so that Katie would have some space and privacy from her four noisy sons.

"I'm not saying chase the man to the altar, Emma." Katie's humor softened her words. "I'm just saying you might want to give him a chance. See what he's about."

"I'll see what happens with all that in time. Right now I know Babe needs me. That will be my primary focus." Emma walked back to the table and sank down into a chair. "You know, it's odd. I know Mack is interested, but my heart isn't saying the same on my end. And on the way over here, Babe reacted to Mack in a way I've never seen her behave before. He tried to draw her into our conversation, but she lashed out at him instead. I don't understand why she doesn't warm up to him." She shrugged. "But then, I don't know why I don't warm up to him, either."

Katie laughed. "Keep your eyes open, pray, and see what happens. This break from the claim is exactly what you need to see what else God has for you and your future. I think great things are about to happen for you."

A ruckus in the yard interrupted their discussion, much to Emma's relief. She knew Katie meant well, but Emma didn't feel comfortable moving any further with the topic of Mack.

"Looks like the men have arrived! Why don't you stay for dinner? You know Hank will want you to join us. I know Jimmy would like it, too. He'll enjoy having Babe around to play with. And you know I'll love to have my coffee partner back. Stay and let us get reacquainted."

"I don't know. I look a mess." Emma gestured at the soiled hem of her blue dress where it had dragged in the mud at the side of the stream. "And my hair. . ."

"Nonsense. Sit there by the window, and I'll do your hair. Your dress is fine. How long has it been since you've been pampered, anyway?"

"About forever," Emma admitted. "But you don't need to cater to me. I'm sure you've worked hard today, too."

"Well, it's been about forever since I've had the pleasure of doing someone else's hair, you know? Let me play. I don't have the luxury of a daughter to doll up. The men won't be in for a while. They have to take care of the stock and clean up themselves. So sit and let me see what I can do."

Emma sat. Her friend kept up a steady stream of chatter without much input from Emma. Emma had to smile at the mental picture she had of a grown-up Babe doing much the same thing. She had no doubt Katie had been lonely of late. "It'll be fun to get together like we used to back when Jimmy and Babe were toddlers."

Katie grunted her answer, her mouth now full of hairpins. She worked in silence for a few minutes, then declared Emma beautiful and pointed her in the direction of the mirror.

Emma instead crossed over to the window and peered out in time to watch Jimmy catapult himself into his father's outstretched arms. Babe stood to the side, a sad smile of longing on her lips as she watched her best friend with her pa. Emma's heart cracked a bit at the wistful expression on her daughter's precious face. Maybe it was time to consider finding a father for Babe. She knew she'd never love anyone else like she'd loved Matthew—or at least she couldn't imagine doing so at this time—so maybe she'd been looking at the whole situation in the wrong way. Maybe she needed to focus on a father for Babe, not a husband for herself.

⟡

Babe was subdued during dinner. Emma knew bedtime wouldn't come soon enough for the child, but she also knew something bothered her daughter.

"I'm not sure a change at the claim is a good idea. Not with Mack, anyway," Hank said as he passed a plate of potatoes. "There might be some better choices to consider."

"Oh now, Hank, that's not a fair comment to make when Mack's not here to defend himself. Why would you say such a thing?" Katie's appalled voice caught Emma's attention and took her thoughts off her daughter.

Emma forced herself to concentrate on the conversation. "Why would you think Mack is a bad idea? He's been partners in the other claim for years, and I've not heard of any problems. He's never been in trouble that I know of. In all due respect, is there something about him you know that I don't?"

Hank measured his words. "I can't put my finger on anything. But there's something, a gut feeling if you will, that makes me ill at ease around him."

"I've not ever had a problem," Emma said, then exchanged a glance with Katie. That wasn't true. She did have that check in her spirit when it came to Mack, but she could never figure out what caused it, so it didn't seem fair to go by that alone when everything else about him added up fine. "Well, maybe I do have reservations. But I have no grounds to base my feelings on. I really don't have any other choice, either."

Hank wiped at his mouth. "I'd love to say I could loan you one of the boys, but I need them to work our area. Winter's almost here, and things will be hard. We need to be ready." His voice tapered off. "I'm sorry. I know life has been hard for you, too. Take one of the boys if you need to. We'll get along."

"I appreciate the offer, but for now I'll let Mack run things. I can always change my mind later. I've already offered him the job."

"I can work your claim, Miss Emma!" Jimmy about bounced off his seat with excitement. "I'm big and strong. I can work."

"I know you'd do a great job, Jimmy. But as I said, I already offered the job to Mack. Let's see how he does, and if he needs help, I'll bring up your name. Deal?"

Babe slammed her fist down on the table. "We don't need help from anybody other than my pa."

Silence bounced off the corners of the room. The adults exchanged startled glances, while Jimmy looked confused.

"You ain't got a pa." He finally broke the silence. "Your pa died a long time ago, and a dead man can't run a claim."

"Jimmy!" Hank's angry voice made everyone jump. "You hush right now."

"But it's true." Jimmy sulked.

Emma felt relief that her child didn't have an exclusive run on attitude. Apparently both children were in a period of testing to see what they could get by with. It must be the age.

Babe surveyed them all with an angelic smile. "I'm not talking about that pa. I'm talking about my new one."

Emma felt her face flame to a bright red. What was she going to do with the child? "You don't have a new pa, Babe. You're talking silly. You need to eat your dinner now so we can get on our way home."

And we can't head home a moment too soon. Surely her daughter didn't mean a reference to Mack. She'd shown him nothing but contempt. No, she couldn't mean him, since when his name was mentioned she'd said they didn't need his help. She'd probably made up a new pa as one of her imaginary friends. "Do you boys mind escorting us part of the way home? I promised Mack we wouldn't walk the trail in the dark alone."

"We'll do better than that. I can hitch up the horses to the wagon, and I'll run you home in that." Hank seemed as anxious to get the talkative Babe on her way as Emma was.

"Mama"—Babe's exasperated breath lifted her hair from her forehead—"I prayed for a new pa. He'll be just like Mr. Jacobs. He'll grab me up and swing me around and call me special names and buy me special treats."

Emma sent up a prayer herself—for a sudden hole to appear, large enough to fall into. The entire Jacobs family stared at her with ill-concealed amusement, waiting for her to clear a way out of this mess. "Finding a pa isn't that easy, Babe. A new pa doesn't just walk up to your front door."

"You told me God could make anything happen." Babe's face contorted into a pout. "Isn't that true anymore?"

"Well, yes, of course it's still true. But we live in the middle of nowhere—"

"Then it will be easier for my pa to know which cabin is ours! He won't have too many places to choose from."

How to explain this to her young daughter? The little girl had no idea of the expectations she had and what they meant. There was no way God would drop a perfect husband on her doorstep. . .now or ever.

three

"Watch, Mama. My papa will do this."

Emma watched as Babe tossed her doll high into the air and missed catching her on the down side. The doll landed with a splat on the grassy dirt in front of the porch.

Babe hurried down to retrieve her baby, holding her close with words of comfort. "Oops." She glanced up at Emma with a regretful sigh. "My papa won't do it that way. Let me try again."

Emma blanched at her daughter's constant chatter about her papa. The little girl, more convinced than ever that her prayer would be answered by a father's appearance on their doorstep, about plowed down anyone who got in her way when a knock sounded at the entry. It didn't even have to be their cabin. It could be Katie's or Liza's, their other neighbor.

But it didn't stop there. She would also run up to other men when they were out and about, looking for her "pa." It could be a complete stranger walking into the general store. Each time, Babe's face would light up and then fall as she surveyed the newest prospect—or victim as he might be called. Not once had she declared she'd found her papa, much to Emma's relief.

The townspeople and their friends found the situation quite amusing. Word had passed around that Babe was in the market for a new papa, and everyone began to offer up suggestions to Emma. Matchmaking attempts had peaked higher than ever. Her nerves were wearing thin.

"Em, can I talk to you for a moment?" Mack walked up the path from the barn. He stood politely on the porch, waiting for an invitation to sit.

Not in the mood for company, especially Mack's company, which would probably start tongues wagging across all of Dakota Territory, she hesitated. She contemplated telling him no, but in the end politeness won out and she motioned for him to take a seat.

"The claim's doing well."

Emma nodded. She supposed his report was necessary, but she wanted him to get to the point.

"We've begun to dig a mine in the hill behind the claim. I've taken a look at the locale, and I think it has huge potential. The men around our claim have offered to get it up and going."

His use of the word "our" raised her hackles. She raised an eyebrow at him, and he quickly caught his mistake. "*Your* claim, of course. Sorry. But while I'm working it every day, I feel a certain ownership. I always keep in mind that if I do a good job, it benefits us all. I only referred to my stake in this, along with yours."

Emma motioned for him to go on. She felt a loss knowing that her claim now had a gaping hole in the hillside behind it. The area that once lay untouched by human hands was being destroyed for man's desire to get rich. She wondered how that could be the right thing to do.

"The mine will allow us to keep working even after the cold weather comes. We'll be partially protected from the elements." He paused as her mind drifted. "Em."

"Emma," she corrected without thinking.

His flat blue eyes narrowed. He corrected himself. "Emma. I think we need to talk."

I'm too tired to talk. I'm worn out through and through. Emma had thought letting go of the claim would refresh her, but instead, with Babe's constant badgering for a father and Mack's frequent hints at wanting marriage, she wanted to curl up and sleep for the next ten years.

"Talk about what?" Her voice was weary, even to her own ears. She knew what was coming and wanted to be anywhere but here. Where had chattering Babe gone when she needed her? Of course, the child still made it clear she had no use for Mack and disappeared as soon as she could when he came around.

"Us." He reached over and took her hand. Emma tried to hide her shudder. "I want you to marry me."

His clammy skin repulsed her. *Lord, if it's in Your will that I marry Mack, please change my heart about him. If it isn't in Your will, show me a sign that I'm on the right track, because I feel very confused.*

She did know that the more Mack was around and the more he immersed himself into her life at the cabin and the claim, the more she resented his presence. She didn't really need a sign from God to know her feelings weren't growing for the man. But she did long for a sign to show her the way out of this mess.

"There is no *us*, Mack." She pulled her hand away and stood to put distance between them. She paced for a moment, trying to gather her thoughts, then perched on the edge of her chair, as far from Mack as physically possible. Though she was tired of putting the man off and fighting his advances, she forced her voice to be gentle. "I'm not ready to have a man in my life, and you know Babe isn't ready, either. I have to think of her. I'm sorry, but I don't want to marry you."

Mack's dull eyes bored into hers. He obviously didn't like to hear that she didn't want to marry him. He made that clearer with each rejection. "Your daughter isn't ready for you to marry because you haven't told her that's how things will be. You need to discipline her and tell her she's a little girl and has no say in things such as this. You give the child too much latitude, and she's spoiled."

Emma's gasp showed her disbelief at the way he'd talked about her daughter. "I'll ask you to please never make a comment like that about my child again." *The audacity!*

"It's true. If she were mine, I'd take a stick to her backside. She has no respect, and I'm tired of her ruining my plans."

"Then it's a sure thing the child will never be yours. *Your* plans are about to crash down around you. How dare you speak of my daughter in that way—or speak to me with such disrespect, for that matter? I'd be best off to send you packing." Emma had again jumped to her feet and now continued to pace across the covered porch's floor. "You work for me, Mack, like it or not. If you can't abide by my standards, you're free to move on to work for someone else."

Mack stood and towered above her, his stance threatening.

Emma had never been so angry in her life. A brief moment of fear flashed through her, but she knew she was only a yell away from a whole barn full of loyal miners who would rush to her side if needed. She watched as he deflated before her eyes. Either he'd realized the same thing, or he could read her face well enough to know she wasn't going to back down.

"I'm sorry." Though his voice sounded dejected, she felt it was an act. "The comments I just made were out of line. It's just. . .I get lonely, and I think we'd make a great partnership. Babe would come around in time."

"I won't marry you, Mack. You need to understand that. I'm not going to change my mind." During the course of their conversation, that fact had come through free and clear. She felt a burden lift from her chest. Her prayer had been answered. "I'd like you to stay on and run the claim, but only if you can live with that fact."

Mack met her gaze and held it steadily before nodding and walking back to the barn without further comment.

❧

Josiah Andrews urged his horse forward, every bit as tired of the journey as was his magnificent stallion, Rocky. The rough terrain made for slow going, and they'd had to wind their way among the rocks, boulders, creeks, and streams that blocked their passage at every turn. If he'd had a straight route through, he'd have arrived in Deadwood weeks ago.

The hot September sun beat down, and Josiah wondered if the temperature always reached such warm extremes this far north or if the adverse weather had been put into place just for him. It seemed that if anything could go wrong on this trek, it had.

He'd been on the trail for years, and though he was on a mission to find a wanted man and to bring him back in, the official visit coincided with a need Josiah had for revenge against a man who had wronged him. He would avenge his brother's death if it was the last thing he did. And what better place to bring his enemy down than Deadwood? One of the most lawless towns around, rumor had it that a man was murdered there almost every day. One more body wouldn't make much of a difference.

A fleeting twinge of guilt passed through him, but Josiah shook it off. Though his motive for capturing the wanted man contradicted his plan for revenge, he felt he had no choice.

"C'mon, ole boy. I see some oats and a comfortable place to sleep in your near future, and in mine, too. Well, maybe not oats for me, but a good hot meal." They'd been riding for weeks, and the trail had warmed considerably as they'd neared Deadwood.

The vegetation grew sparser as they approached the outskirts of town, a sure sign they were close to their destination. Everything would be perfect as long as no one recognized who he was. At least before he caught his quarry. He'd analyze the sins of his plan after the fact. Until then, anything could go as far as he was concerned.

The town bustled with activity as Josiah rode in. He took his time, perusing it from one end to the other. He needed to be familiar with the layout. It seemed mostly filled with men, and several of the women he could see were definitely not the type he'd ever bring home to his mother. Though no church could be seen, plenty of gambling, drinking, and dancing establishments lined the rough dirt road.

Josiah urged his horse forward to a small hotel and tied him to the post out front. He removed his satchel from the saddle and mounted the rickety stairs that led to the hotel porch. A woman leaned against the doorway of a nearby saloon and propositioned him, but he ignored her and pushed into the stuffy interior.

Rooms opened off both sides of the foyer—one obviously a sitting room of sorts and the other, based on the clink and clatter of dishes, the dining room. A central staircase led up the right wall, and a counter wrapped along the wall to the left.

While Josiah stood and took in the hotel's floor plan, a bored man sat behind the counter and watched the action taking place outside, a bonus for a man who wanted to remain unrecognized. "Can I help you?"

"I need a room." Josiah plunked a few bills down on the counter. This would be the perfect place to lay low. "And I'll want a hot bath."

The man consulted a ledger, picked up a key from behind him, and handed it over to Josiah. "Top of the stairs and to the left. Your room is the second door, again on the left. Stable's out back."

Good, a room at the front of the building with a view of the street. Josiah wondered if his luck had finally changed. He could watch for his quarry, and no one would be the wiser.

᧞

The bath and clean clothes did a lot for Josiah's disposition as he headed down to eat a late lunch. The room clanged with noise, and he wished for the dinner companions of the civilized towns he'd visited previously.

Here the tables were packed with miners, most with no manners at all. Local girls swarmed the room, talking to the men while they ate. Josiah picked a small table in the corner and put on his surliest face, hoping everyone would leave him alone.

A middle-aged woman hurried to his table. "Hi, I'm Sarah. I'm sorry if you've been waiting long. I didn't notice you slip in over here." She was out of breath from rushing around.

"I haven't been here but a few moments," Josiah reassured her. This woman would be perfect for his questioning. He placed his order, relieved to see that the room had begun to clear of most guests. They meandered outside and went about their daily business. Josiah had a feeling that he hadn't picked the quietest place in town for his stay. But from the looks of it, there wouldn't be any other place less populated. He'd have to use a pillow over his head to get a good night of sleep, if the number of saloons was an indication.

Sarah returned with his pork chop and potatoes. The town might be rough and rugged, but if the aroma of the meal held its promise, the food would be well worth the stay.

"Sarah, I'm looking for an old friend. I'm thinking maybe you can help me out with locating him." Josiah held his breath in anticipation after giving her the name. His effort finally, after all these months, had paid off. After Sarah spouted off directions on where to find the man he'd hunted, he couldn't hide his smile. Not even a miner, and he'd struck the mother lode.

Though his appetite hadn't diminished, he hurried through the meal, ready to get back on his horse and track his brother's killer.

❧

Emma placed the last clean dish onto the shelf and wiped her damp hands on a towel. Upon hearing a noise from out front, she hesitated, trying to place the sound. She hurried across the cabin's floor at the approach of a horse. She hadn't expected anyone at this time of day, and her friends Katie and Liza always walked when they came to visit. The men would eventually be back from the claims, but not for hours.

Babe slept on her small bed behind Emma as she peeked out the window to see a stranger approach. Hefting her rifle from its resting place on the mantel, Emma quietly lifted the latch and went out to meet the stranger.

He stopped the horse a safe distance away.

"Who are you, and what do you want?" she called out to him, hoping her voice wouldn't carry inside to wake Babe. "State your business or leave."

The stranger raised his hands. "I don't mean you any harm. I just have a few questions about the men who board here."

Emma moved down the stairs but kept her rifle aimed at his chest. From where she stood, she could see he had a gun in a holster by his side. She couldn't tell the make from this distance. But it wouldn't matter if he was a sharp-shooter. Her rifle would never be a match for his gun, especially if he was a quick draw. "What kind of questions? The boarders here don't look for trouble, and they don't find any, either. They're all good men."

"I'm sure they are. I don't mean to make trouble, either." He forced his mount a few steps closer, then swung down from the saddle.

She couldn't help but notice the strong muscles of his legs as they rippled from the movement. Her heart skipped a few beats. Now that he'd come closer, she saw that he had to be the handsomest man she'd ever laid eyes on. Wide shoulders filled out his off-white shirt and complemented his slim hips and long, lean legs. Black hair tumbled over his forehead in disarray. But his good looks were marred by the underlying current of anger that simmered deep within his dark brown eyes.

"Don't come any closer." The rifle had drooped in her hold as she openly perused the appealing stranger. Catching herself, she swung it back up against her shoulder. She started to say she had a small child inside whom she needed to protect, but then thought better than to offer him the information if he had ill reasons for being there. "I won't hesitate to shoot."

The man had the audacity to chuckle. "I don't doubt that you will. I know you have a child, and I'd feel the same caution if I were in your place."

So much for keeping Babe a secret. "Who are you?"

"Forgive my lack of manners. The name is Josiah. Josiah Andrews. I'm new in town."

"You and every other man on the street." Newcomers poured into the town every day and had ever since the first nugget of gold was found. Emma had been there longer than most. They'd settled into the area before the first gold was discovered, which accounted for their great location and claim.

"I'd like to know the names of the men you have staying here."

"And I'd still like to know a good reason for me to tell you."

The man stepped closer and measured her with his glance. She wondered if he liked what he saw. Did he find her as appealing as she found him? Mentally shaking her head at her silliness, she warned herself not to fall into a ridiculous fantasy like Babe's.

"I'm looking for an old friend."

"What's his name? If he's here, I'll have him look you up. . .back in town." She hoped her meaning came through clearly—she didn't want the stranger lingering around.

"Mack Jeffries. Do you know of him?"

Just then the front door of the cabin burst open Babe-style, and the little girl hurtled out onto the porch.

"This must be Babe."

Emma's attention was torn. "Babe, stay back. Don't come off the porch."

Josiah took advantage of her attention moving away from him and stepped several feet closer.

"Stop! Both of you." Emma turned her focus back to Josiah even as she heard Babe's dainty footsteps bouncing down the stairs. Neither person listened to her admonition to stop.

"Hello, sweetheart." Josiah greeted Babe with a soft voice. His entire countenance changed, as if he were viewing an angel in the flesh.

"Hello, Papa," Babe responded, racing past Emma before she could stop her.

Emma watched in disbelief as her daughter flew into the surprised man's arms. The little girl buried her face in his shoulder before peeking up at her mother. "See? I told you God would send my papa to our doorstep."

Emma felt herself beginning to panic. Whatever the man's purpose, her most valuable treasure now rested in his arms.

four

"Unhand my daughter and you might ride out of here with your life." Emma motioned with the rifle, though she knew the movement had lost its effect with Babe's arrival on the scene. She'd lowered it to point at the ground and held it loosely in one hand. So far, in all honesty, the man had given her no reason to think he'd come to cause them harm. But she couldn't take any chances.

"Me unhand her?" Josiah looked down at the child who was clinging to him. "And how will you manage to shoot me with your daughter between your gun and my chest?"

Babe raised her head in horror. "You can't shoot my papa when he's only just arrived!"

Tired, out of patience, and wanting the man gone and Babe safely tucked away into the cabin, Emma pinned her daughter with a glare. "He's not your papa, Babe. He's a stranger. Now hop down like a good girl and get up here on the porch by your mama where I can keep you safe."

Babe ignored her and buried her face against his. "He smells good, Mama. Come over and sniff his neck."

"I will not!" Emma could feel the multiple shades of color as they flew up her cheeks. "Babe Delaney, get off that man right now."

"Are you sure? I have another side just for you." The stranger had the nerve to stand there and grin.

Emma's rebellious thoughts noted that it was a very charming grin.

"And I can't say I've ever heard words quite like that come out of a mother's mouth while her daughter is in her arms."

And what was that supposed to mean? Did he have a lot of females caught in his clutches by their mothers? Emma gasped, and her hand flew to her heart. She couldn't believe the man would toy with her like this. First he rode up looking dangerous—*and extremely handsome,* her traitorous thoughts added—and now he stood there gently clasping her wayward daughter in his arms like some kind of pink-clad porcelain doll. And his teasing words added fuel to Babe's papa dreams.

"Well, we obviously have some more work to do in the decorum and how-to-act-around-men area of life."

"Please smell his neck, Mama. You might like him and want him to stay."

"As I was saying. . ." This whole situation had become utterly ridiculous, and Emma had lost all control—of her daughter, the man who stood before her, and her life. "Babe, he's not a sweet little puppy you just decide to invite into your home." That didn't sound right. She sighed. "Please put my daughter down."

Josiah raised both arms in mock surrender. Babe remained where she was, hanging from his neck, hugging him for all she was worth. "With all due respect, ma'am. It's a long way down to the ground, and she might fall."

"Then bring her up on the porch. I give up." She watched as he secured the child in his arms.

The man tipped his wide-brimmed hat and sauntered

past her onto the porch, where he dropped gratefully into a chair.

Babe repositioned herself and snuggled against his chest. Her brown eyes were huge as she stared up at him, and her fluffy blond hair framed her face in a most adorable way. Emma watched, entranced, as the anger disappeared from the stranger's eyes when he smiled down at the impish child in his arms.

He glanced up at Emma, and his mouth quirked up on one side. He had a dimple. "I hate to impose, but it's a long ride out here. Do you think you could fetch me a drink? I'd get it myself, but. . ." He motioned to Babe, who now appeared to be asleep.

"I'm not leaving you alone out here with my daughter."

"If I meant you harm, I'd have injured you already. It would have been nothing to hop on my horse and take off with her when she first jumped into my arms. And to further put your mind at ease, I came out here looking for Mack at the recommendation of Sarah over at the hotel. She knows I've headed this way, and if there's any foul play, I'm the first person they'd be after."

Emma had to admit that what he said made sense. "Let me get your water, and then you can tell me what you want with Mack."

She grabbed a mug and dipped it in the water pail before hurrying back out the open door. Josiah hadn't moved from his place in the chair, but with his head tipped back against the wood of the front wall of the cabin, he appeared to be asleep.

Emma stood staring and felt a tug in her heart. Babe looked so sweet cuddled in the man's strong arms. She also looked incredibly tiny. She wanted a papa so badly. It wasn't fair hers had been taken from her at such a young age. Emma didn't know how they'd get through this afternoon without breaking Babe's heart.

The man opened one eye and peeked out at her. "That my water?"

"Oh, I'm sorry, yes. Here." She handed it over, embarrassed to have been caught staring. She settled in a chair across from him. "Now, about your reasons for asking to see Mack..."

"It's personal."

"That's it? I'm supposed to hand over a man with no questions asked? Is he a friend?"

"At one time."

"But not anymore?"

"Nope. Not anymore."

They were getting nowhere fast. "He runs my claim."

Josiah sat up so quickly, Emma thought he'd drop Babe. But instead his arms gripped her protectively. "He's running your claim? For how long? Is that where I'll find him now?"

"I don't see how any of this is business of yours. You don't want to tell me the least little bit of reason why you're here, but you expect me to spill my life story to you?"

"That pretty much sums it up. There are things you don't need to know. But you shouldn't trust Mack so easily."

Emma grew tired of the man and his puzzling comments. "You have no idea how easy or hard it was for me to trust him. He's been a family friend for years—first to my husband, and after his passing, to my daughter and myself."

Emma wasn't sure why she defended Mack with such intensity when she'd been having her own doubts of late, but it probably had more to do with defending her choices. If the man questioned her choice in trusting Mack, he questioned her ability to reason in general, and for some silly reason, it was important to Emma to have Josiah's respect. It also seemed to be important because if she'd been wrong to trust Mack, her entire future stood at risk.

ஜ

Josiah studied the woman before him and wondered what thoughts were passing through her mind. She looked torn, as if she wanted to help but didn't know the best way.

"If you tell me where to find Mack, I'll take it from there," he said. "You don't need to be involved. I'll take care of my business with him, and you can go on your way."

"He's at the claim. It's quite a walk up that path over near the barn, and it will be dark before you arrive. It would be best if you waited until tomorrow to do your business with him. I'll tell him you came by."

"Right, and by tomorrow he'll be long gone. I can't— won't—take that chance. I've searched for him way too long to lose him now." He saw a shudder pass through Emma and felt bad for scaring her. "Look, I don't mean to bring you an added burden. I'll do my best to make sure our business doesn't interfere with you here at the cabin or in any way harm your little girl. But I have to confront Mack, and it has to be today. You have my word that I won't hurt him."

He still couldn't read the emotions that passed across her face. His previous words startled him as much as they appeared to startle her. How could he have promised not to hurt Mack? His whole intent upon coming here was to collect the ultimate price from the man. Mack had caused Josiah's brother's death, and he fully planned to exact the same payment from Mack. He felt a scowl cross his face and fought to control his emotions. It wouldn't do to frighten Emma.

"If you've searched for him for years and he's no longer a friend, I have to assume you have a vendetta against him. Am I correct?" Her brown eyes, identical to her daughter's, bored into him. "I rely on Mack heavily. If something happens to him, I don't know what I'll do."

"There are other men by the dozens who'd love to take over your claim. You said so yourself. New men come to town every day."

"Yes, but I don't want to give my claim away. I want someone to partner with me in running it. I took care of the claim myself up until a few weeks ago. It's become too hard with Babe along. She's at a very precocious age, and I was worried about her safety."

"So I can see." Josiah's warm laugh drifted over to Emma, and she looked surprised.

She motioned at the child in his arms. "You seem comfortable with her. Do you have a child of your own?"

Josiah felt the surprise register on his face at her question. "No. I've not been around children much at all. This one took me by surprise."

Emma appeared startled, then contemplative. "Hmm."

He wondered what the reaction meant. He then shook off the thought. He had one goal to follow—not counting his capture of the wanted man in town—and he needed to focus on that goal, not the two unexpected women who were taking his heart captive as he watched.

The guilt reared its ugly head again. If he succeeded in his plans with Mack, these two would be left high and dry. There would be no one to run the claim. He pushed the thought away. That wasn't his problem. She wasn't safe with Mack running the claim anyway. Ultimately, he'd do her a favor by ridding them of the man. His plan for Mack would be a blessing to the woman and child in the long run; they just might not ever know it. He felt sorrow that they'd not see it that way, but he knew his plan was definitely for the best.

❧

"I need to be on my way. Do you want me to lay her down inside or hand her off to you?"

Emma stood and reached for her daughter. Babe had napped long enough that there was no way she'd sleep through his laying her down. Emma didn't feel comfortable with the man entering her private quarters, either. She braced herself for the wrath of Babe.

"No! I want to stay with you, Papa!"

Emma smirked. She'd been right. Let the man deal with the little girl, since he'd been so smug earlier when her daughter had catapulted into his arms. He threw Emma a look begging for help, but she merely shrugged. She watched as he lowered himself to one knee and placed Babe on her feet.

"I have to go now, but I enjoyed meeting you."

"Papas don't just leave their children. I want you to stay here."

He again looked up at Emma, confusion apparent on his face.

"She's been praying for a papa, and she's sure one will be sent to her. You arrived, and. . ." Emma waved her hand as if that explained it all. She didn't want to go into the whole sordid mess.

"Oh." He stared at the little girl. "I'm sure you'll find that papa someday soon. If I see him, I'll tell him to head this way, all right?"

Babe's face screwed up, and tears gathered in her eyes. "But you're the one He sent."

"I'm here to finish a plan put into place long ago, not to be a pa, Babe. I enjoyed meeting you, and you're a daughter that would make any father proud. I'm sorry it won't be me." He stood.

Babe clutched his leg. "But I don't want *any* father; I want you!"

Emma decided she'd let the man go through enough torture to get even for his interrupting her afternoon. She peeled a crying Babe from his thigh. "Come along, Babe. Let the man be on his way."

Josiah sent her a grateful look and started down the stairs. "I appreciate the water and the information."

"You're welcome." Emma stopped short of calling out that he was welcome back anytime. She also felt sad as the man walked out of their life. What a crazy thought!

He stopped near his horse and looked back at them with a strange expression. He shook his head as if to clear it and readied himself to ride.

"Papa!" Babe broke out of Emma's grasp and flew down the stairs.

Josiah turned around to see her barreling toward him and stepped forward to meet her, swinging her up into a circle and spinning her around. He set her back down on the ground and knelt down to her level again. "I tell you what, baby doll. If your mama says it's okay, I'll come back through here before I leave town. I'll stop off to say good-bye."

Babe couldn't speak but nodded.

Josiah glanced up at Emma, and she nodded, too. What else could she do? She knew inside she wanted to see him again as much as her daughter did. And with that spin in the air and endearing name—which Babe would have railed at Mack for—he'd just firmly ensconced himself into Babe's heart as her pa.

Emma led Babe inside, so flustered at her daughter's enamored chatter and her belief that Jesus had indeed led the man to their doorstep to become her pa that it took her precious minutes to realize Josiah had left by way of the trail that led to the claim.

She flew into action, knowing that his intentions weren't the best when it came to Mack and that she'd unwillingly— or willingly, led by Josiah's charm—directly placed Mack into danger. "Come, Babe, we have to hurry and get up to the claim." She gathered up Babe's boots, dusted off her dirty stockings, and shoved the leather on the little girl's feet.

"Ouch, you're hurting me, Mama!" Babe fought her, and Emma forced herself to slow down and be gentler.

"Your feet are growing again. They barely fit into your boots. I'll have to buy you a bigger pair next time we're in town."

"Oh, new boots! Can we go now? I want my papa to see them."

"No, we need to get to the claim." Emma didn't even bother correcting her daughter. She contemplated dropping Babe off at Katie's on the way but knew she couldn't afford the wasted minutes it would take to do so. And Katie would be full of questions that Emma didn't have time to answer, or even have answers for! Babe would fuel the fire, too, when happily telling Katie and Jimmy that her father had sure enough arrived on their doorstep and had swung her around and called her baby doll. Emma would never get out from under their inquisition after that.

She grabbed Babe's hand, hustled out the door, and took off at a run. She slowed when she heard her daughter's labored breathing. Bending down, she took her daughter upon her back and moved as quickly as she could with the heavy load. She didn't believe Josiah had told her the truth about not hurting Mack. His life hung in the balance. She had to make it to the claim in time.

five

Emma could hear the raised voices even as she neared the opening in the trail. Out of breath, she set Babe down and walked over to Ben Parson. "Could you take Babe over to your claim and distract her while I find out what this is all about?"

Ben shook his head even as he reached for the little girl. Emma knew the motion had to do with his frustration with the men, not with caring for Babe.

"I don't know what's gotten into them boys," he said. "It seems things usually stay pretty calm up here compared to the problems at the newer claims in other areas."

"Well, the tall one *is* a newcomer, and apparently he's bent on shaking things up over our way. Thanks for keeping Babe occupied. I appreciate it."

She watched as Babe skipped along at Ben's heels, already telling him her newest story. Emma cringed as she heard the words "my papa" in the conversation. Poor Ben was already getting an earful. Emma would have a lot of explaining to do when she returned to collect her daughter.

Ben handed Babe a lightweight gold pan he kept handy for her visits and hunkered down beside the towheaded waif. He glanced over at Emma with a smirk and eyebrows raised in question.

Emma rolled her eyes and turned to push herself through the crowd.

Mack stood at the side of the stream, and Josiah towered over him on the hill above. A gaping hole, the new mine entrance, loomed behind him. Emma couldn't make out their words. Though obviously angry, the men spoke in hushed voices.

Just as she broke through the last wall of men, Mack picked up a shovel and held it high over his head.

"Mack, no!" Her cry was lost in the scuffle.

She watched in shock and horror as Josiah glanced up, registered Mack's intent, and shoved the other man, hard. Mack went down. Josiah uttered more words, and Mack flew to his feet.

Josiah seemed to want a discussion, whereas Mack preferred a fistfight. Josiah's hands splayed out in front of him in a gesture of backing off, but Mack swung at him and connected with his right jaw.

"No." Emma's voice was but a whisper now. She didn't waste the effort of yelling when she knew the men wouldn't hear her even if she stood two inches from them.

Josiah's head snapped to the left. He stumbled but somehow managed to keep his footing. He bent and placed his hands on his knees as he fought the stars that had to be circling his head. Emma knew the effect because she'd experienced the same when hit in the jaw by an out-of-control horse a few years back.

A small trail of blood poured from his lip, and he swiped at it with his sleeve, oblivious to the bright red that stained his off-white shirt. He glanced over at Mack and said a few more words.

Emma looked at Mack for the first time. With his hair in disarray, he looked like he'd had his share of hits before

Emma's arrival. But it was his eyes that sent a shiver of fear coursing through her body. They were wild, the eyes of a man who wasn't in his right mind. Had he always been this way and hidden it well? Or was this a side of Mack that came out when he was crossed? She well remembered his anger over her refusal of marriage. She didn't know how this day would end, but she was sure she didn't want Mack running her claim any longer, nor did she want him on her property.

She moved forward as the men stared at each other. Josiah dropped his head again, letting down his guard, and Mack took advantage and threw two more punches. Josiah dropped to his knees. Emma's hand flew up to cover her mouth. Bile rose in her throat, and she felt like she was about to be sick.

"I told you, I'm not going to fight, Mack. You need to come with me. A fight won't change the way things are. There're legal ways to deal with this."

"I'll die before I come with you. You just want to get me away from these witnesses so you can kill me." Mack's glazed eyes stared at the gathered crowd.

Josiah's voice was labored. "No, if I wanted to kill you, I'd do it now. Here in front of God and everyone. It's what you deserve, and it's what you'll get if I start with one swing."

Emma saw Mack's thought process in motion before Josiah had another chance to defend himself. Mack reached for the shovel, and everything slowed down in Emma's mind. She saw the shovel arc up. She saw Josiah reach for his gun. But before he could connect with the handle, the tool connected with the side of his head with a sickening *thud*.

The crowd stood motionless for a moment, and then all surged forward. Though Josiah was the stranger, he'd done nothing to instigate the violence against him. At least not that Emma could see. These were good men, her neighbors, and they didn't stand for an unfair fight. No one had expected to see the damage and anger Mack had just shown.

"Josiah!" Emma dropped to her knees beside his still body. She hoped Ben was keeping Babe from seeing this. "Josiah, can you hear me?"

Blood poured from the gash in the side of his head. Someone pressed a handkerchief into her hand, and she placed it against the flow.

"Josiah, you have to wake up. Stay with us. We'll get you help." She looked up at Phil Duggin.

"There's no way we can get him to town in this condition, ma'am. The ride would be too much for him. The best we could probably do is to get him down off this hill." He scratched his head as if the action would improve his thinking. "We need to get him stable."

"Take him to my place." Emma was as surprised as the men around her when the words popped out of her mouth. But the truth was, it was her claim and her worker who had caused him to get in this mess—even if Josiah had ignored her request to wait until another day—and she felt responsible for the man.

She looked around. "Where's Mack?"

The men glanced at each other, and finally a voice from the back of the crowd called out, "He took off through the far woods like he had a bear on his trail."

Emma didn't want to think the worst of Mack. He *had*

been there for her during the past two years, but if he wasn't guilty of whatever Josiah had claimed, why had he reacted with such rage and then run off?

"Did any of you hear what the actual argument was about?"

Mutters of denial drifted around her.

"No, ma'am."

"Too far away."

"Stream too noisy."

"They talked in quiet voices until those last few exchanges at the end."

"Okay," she finally said. "We'll take him to my cabin. Someone needs to ride out for Doc." Emma gently pulled the handkerchief away, relieved to see the bleeding had slowed. "Let's get going."

"I'll go for Doc." Phil headed down the trail.

"Stop by my place and take one of the horses. You'll get there faster, even if it's a bit out of your way to town."

"Good idea. Will do." He hurried off down the trail with a few of her boarders following along to help.

Emma stepped back, and several men moved forward to take her place. They secured Josiah for the trek back to the cabin by placing him on a heavy blanket they could carry between them. She hurried over to snag Babe so they could be on their way.

Though in a hurry to keep up with Josiah, she started to update Ben on the situation, but he waved her away. "I'll catch the news from the menfolk. You go on ahead. But take good care of the man. According to Babe, he has an important place in your lives." His eyes twinkled with his teasing.

A small smile formed on her lips against her will. "He's a stranger, Mr. Parson. He has no place in our lives other than my trying to keep him alive until Doc can reach our cabin."

"I hear ya, ma'am. I hear ya." He tipped his hat at her and shooed her off toward home. "But I have to say I witnessed a good part of that confrontation, and the man was trying not to get into a physical altercation with Mack. It takes a good man to refuse to fight when fighting commences against him."

"Or a coward," young Bill Mercer jeered from across the stream.

Ben measured him with a glance, and his expression showed he found the younger man lacking. "That man is no coward. I wouldn't go up face-to-face with him for anything. His anger simmered under the show of patience, but I wouldn't want to be on the receiving end of a bad situation with him. He's one fierce man, and why he didn't give Mack more is beyond me."

"He promised me he wouldn't hurt Mack." Emma broke in on the conversation. "I don't know why, because his intent came across loud and clear even back at the cabin, but somewhere in the conversation he felt compelled to make me that promise. I guess he kept it, huh?"

"Well, little missy, maybe you ought to take your daughter's prayers and beliefs to heart. Looks to me like Someone bigger than all of us might have a plan here."

"Oh no. No way. This is not what Babe thinks. I'm sure Josiah, er, Mr. Andrews, had every intention of coming up here for no good, but for whatever reason, he decided not to make a public scene with his vendetta." She was glad Babe had wandered out of hearing range to pick wildflowers and missed the conversation.

Walking the few feet away to collect her daughter, she took Babe's hand and turned her toward the trail. "Now, if you don't mind, I'll be off to see to the man and prepare him to go with Doc as soon as he can get by to pick him up. I don't want him at my place a moment longer than he needs to be."

&

"What do you mean he can't travel yet? He has to. He can't stay here!" Emma heard the dismay she felt as it flowed through her words. What did Doc think, telling her the man had to stay put where he was? He lay in her cabin. . . in her bed! He couldn't possibly stay.

"Emma, I know you heard me loud and clear when I explained his condition. He has a concussion. If we move him now, he'll never make it to town alive. And the noise there won't be conducive to his recovery, either. Out here he has you to care for him, the fresh air, and quiet."

Emma raised an eyebrow and glanced at Babe, who sat outside the front window singing at the top of her lungs about "a papa come to stay."

"Well, maybe not quiet, but it still beats the ruckus he'd deal with in town." Doc had the nerve to chuckle at Babe's choice of song. "She's excited over this, isn't she? You don't want to break the young girl's heart, do you?"

"I don't want to build her hopes, either, and this man isn't gonna be her papa. She needs to accept that. I can't take care of him." Emma smoothed the cover even as she said it. *Way to show my reluctance to help.*

Doc stared at her for a moment and sighed. "I see your

situation and understand your reticence. If you want me to move him, if you feel in any way he's a threat to you, I'll take him along whatever the result may be. We can pack him on blankets and drive slow, but. . ."

"But if he dies, his blood's on my hands right along with Mack's?" Emma let her breath out in a huff. Doc knew she'd never send the man to his death. He knew exactly the words to use on her.

"I didn't say that." The glimmer in Doc's eyes matched Ben's earlier twinkle exactly. It seemed as if everyone had been let in on a secret that she alone didn't know. "I'm just telling you how it is. You've always wanted me to be direct with you."

"Yes, when it comes to Babe's health and well-being. I don't want you to mollycoddle me when she's sick just because you worry I can't take the truth. But this. . ." She waved a hand at the man in her bed. "How am I to care for him? I'm single and a widow. It isn't right."

"Sometimes life and death don't worry about propriety." He moved to pack his bag, then picked up his hat from the chair near the door. He stopped with his hand on the latch. "Seems you could get one of the men from the barn to help with any needs you might have with his care. I know a couple of them have right colorful pasts and are used to caring for gunshot wounds and the victims of those bullets."

"My men? How is it you know this and I don't? Most of them have been boarding here for two years. I didn't know any of them had that type of past!" Emma wondered now what she'd been subjecting her daughter—and herself—to by keeping these men around. "Maybe it would be best if

I asked them all to leave. I sure had Mack pegged wrong."

"Sure, if you want to care for Josiah alone. Send 'em all packing."

Emma caught Doc's insinuation. If she sent them on their way, she'd have no one to help with Josiah's care. Not a good idea. At least not now. She'd keep them around until Josiah improved enough to care for himself. Meanwhile, she'd spend a bit more time with the men, asking about their lives, and see what they were about.

"Emma, if the men were a threat, you'd have known it by now. Those men would do anything for you. They're all patients of mine and rave about what a wonderful woman you are. You have nothing to worry about with any of them." He hesitated. "If there were to be concerns about any one of them, I'd have bet my money on Mack. There always seemed to be something simmering under the surface when it came to him."

So much for my discernment. She'd thought him the safest of them all. . .and the most trustworthy. But now that she thought about it, that was mostly because of her deceased husband's faith in him. "Thanks for sharing, Doc. I'll see you in the morning, then?"

"Yes, and don't worry. I've got him stabilized, and there isn't anything to do but keep an eye on him and follow the few instructions I left for you in case he comes to before my return." He pulled the door open, and Babe's happy squeal carried through the opening. "If you'd feel better, have the men sleep in shifts on the porch. That way someone will always be near if you need him."

"And what if a stray bullet comes for one of them while he's on my porch?" Emma's smile gave away her teasing.

But truth be told, she couldn't tell Doc which man would possibly be used to bullets tearing around him, so she didn't feel very qualified to pick which ones should come to her rescue if needed. She'd rather stick it out by herself. She briefly considered asking Doc to escort Babe over to Katie's or Liza's but quickly brushed the thought away. Her daughter didn't need any more notions about Josiah's role in their lives put into her head, but if Babe left, Emma would be alone with Josiah. That wouldn't do at all.

Emma couldn't admit to herself whether she feared him or her feelings toward him more. She'd simply have to nurse the stranger back to health and send him on his way. She could handle this. He surely wouldn't be around for much more than a day.

six

Josiah tried to open his eyes, but they wouldn't cooperate. He turned his head, and a shooting arrow of pain throbbed through his head. He forced back the darkness that tried to recapture him, but before he could register any information about where he was or what had happened to him, a warm cloak of unconsciousness embraced him and again wiped away the pain.

It seemed minutes, but Josiah could tell hours had passed when he next regained consciousness. Earlier, when he'd tried to peer out from between his lashes, bright light filled the room. Now semidarkness cloaked the area, allowing Josiah to briefly take in his surroundings. Nothing felt familiar.

A scuffling noise to his left had him turning his head in that direction. He moaned as a burst of pain shot across the side of his head. He squeezed his eyes shut to block it out. When the wave of accompanying nausea passed, he again forced his eyes partly open and met a brown-eyed gaze inches from his own.

"Mama, he's awake!" Babe's gleeful shout caused Josiah to squeeze his eyes shut.

"Shush, child," a voice chastised from across the room. "You'll scare him to death." The voice moved closer, its tone soft as velvet. "Now hurry off to bed as you were told. Mr. Andrews will still be here when you wake up."

Josiah waited a moment but didn't hear the little girl leave. He opened his eyes and peered out at her. She still nestled almost nose to nose with him, with both elbows against his pillow and her chin balanced upon folded hands. "Hello, Papa." She gave him an angelic smile.

A chuckle escaped Josiah's lips. He didn't have the energy to correct her. "Hello, baby doll." His raspy voice made him wonder how long he'd been unconscious.

So he was at Emma's place?

He heard a growl of frustration that had to have come from Emma. "Babe, he's *not* your papa. You have to stop this nonsense! Now scoot on over to bed."

Babe obeyed with a huff.

Josiah watched as Emma tucked her daughter snugly into bed. He could hear the soft prayers of mother and child before Emma dropped a kiss against Babe's forehead and patted the blanket that covered her. "Sweet dreams. See you in the morning." She stood watching her daughter for a moment then turned to hurry over to him.

His pulse picked up. He didn't know if it was from wariness over her feelings about his being there, excitement that a beautiful brown-eyed blond headed his way, or frustration that he lay helpless in her bed, weak as a baby. He never had been one to laze around, and he didn't take kindly to people coddling him. He tried to rise to a sitting position, but the blinding pain quickly put him flat on his back.

"Not ready to jump out of bed, I see." Emma's soft voice held a glimmer of humor. "You need to stay still and rest until morning."

Josiah didn't need to be told now that he'd tried to sit up.

"How long have I been sick?" His scratchy throat caused him to cough. He went stiff to fight off the pain. He heard the sound of water being poured into a glass, and then Emma's soft fingers eased under his head, urging him to lean forward and take a sip.

The soothing water flowed down his parched throat, but he couldn't stop the awareness of her touch. He pulled back, motioning that he'd had enough. "So how long?" His voice sounded stronger, not so rough.

"Since yesterday afternoon." He felt his expression change from confusion to frustration. "Mack hit you with a shovel and knocked you out cold before taking off into the woods. No one's seen him since."

"Argh." Josiah tried to keep his voice down, but he couldn't believe he'd let Mack slip through his fingers again. Not this time, when he'd been so close. "He's not come back for his things?"

"No."

Josiah tried to rise from the bed again. Emma pushed him down. Her no-nonsense touch seared through his blanket, firm enough to make clear she'd have nothing to do with his trying to leave. She picked up a small glass bottle from beside the bed and measured out a dose. "Take this. Doc said it will help with the pain."

He turned his mouth away from the medicine. "I don't need anything. I need my wits about me."

"You can take that up with Doc in the morning, but for now, he said he wanted you to have it. If you don't take it, you'll toss and turn all night in pain and keep us all awake. Stop being difficult and do as the doctor ordered."

He glared at her, but her tone allowed no argument. Now

he knew how Babe felt, with her little huff of frustration. He opened his mouth and took the bitter liquid. "There's nothing wrong with my arms, ya know. I could have done that myself."

"I'm sure you're perfectly capable. But we don't want to waste any, and I'm here to care for you. Let me do my job."

"So about Mack—would you know if he returned?"

"The men are watching and will detain him if he comes close again. But only if I give them good reason. They aren't going to hold him until you're better just so you can run over and start another altercation with him."

"I didn't. . ." His voice tapered off. He couldn't really deny he'd started the fight, if only by his presence. "I don't want trouble. I never intended to be a burden to you."

"So you're not going to tell me what this is all about?" Emma pulled a chair up close so their words wouldn't wake Babe.

He stared at the woman while trying to gather his thoughts. *Breathtaking.* The word popped up from nowhere but definitely described the beauty sitting before him. He understood why every bachelor in the surrounding Deadwood area seemed to board in her barn. Her brown eyes radiated warmth, and tendrils of blond hair curled in a beguiling way at each side of her cheeks before tapering down to tease her neck. The neck—along with her cheeks—that now flooded with color at his blatant perusal.

"Sorry." He moved his attention to the lamp behind her. "I'll tell you, but not now." He forced a yawn and hoped she'd believe the tired act and leave him alone until he could better focus on his explanation. In this state of half wakefulness, he didn't trust his words not to betray him.

When she'd asked her question just now, he thought she referred to his staring. He'd almost blurted out that he found her attractive enough that he would consider staying if he thought he had a chance to win her heart. Instead, he caught himself at the last moment after realizing her question was aimed at his issue with Mack.

She laid her cool hand against his forehead, and he closed his eyes at the soothing sensation.

"You have no fever, so I'm hoping the risk of infection is going away. I'm sure you need more rest, though, so sleep and we'll talk in the morning." Her hand lingered.

He wanted to beg her to keep it there, tell her he'd be well before she knew it if she kept her healing touch against his skin. But she moved it moments later, and he opened his eyes to watch as she scooted her chair back away from the side of his bed.

"Doc stopped by yesterday afternoon and again this morning. He said the wound looked well and that he expects you to have a full recovery within a few days. As soon as you get up and around, you can move out to the barn with the other men. You're welcome to stay as long as you like out there."

Josiah suddenly decided he'd not wish for a fast recovery. He liked being in the homey warmth of Emma's place. "What wound do you refer to?"

"You have a gash where the shovel connected."

"Ah. Left side of my head." The reason for the shooting pain when he'd tried to look over at Babe.

"Yes. Doc stitched it up and said today that it's healing well. But it might bleed if you move around too much, so he wants you to stay in bed until he gives his approval for you to be up and around."

"If he insists."

Emma smiled as if she knew his intentions.

Josiah admitted he wasn't the type to languish in bed if not completely necessary, but if Doc said he had to stay. . . who was he to argue? He fought to hide his own grin.

"Somehow you don't strike me as the kind to take a doctor's orders that seriously."

"The company's good here, and service seems to be okay. I'll do my best to endure." He quirked his mouth up in the smirk women seemed to love and watched as Emma responded by rolling her eyes before pulling the curtain between his bed and Babe's.

He heard her walk around the room, her soft breath blowing out the lamp that burned on the mantel before finally settling into the far side of Babe's bed with a creak of the wood frame.

Tired though he was, Josiah had a feeling he'd be hard pressed to get a wink of sleep with the beautiful woman so close to his space. If he had to crawl out, it might be best if he moved to the barn. The two ladies in the cabin had him enchanted in a most endearing way.

❧

Emma snuggled close to her young daughter on the small bed meant for one. She'd placed Babe between her and the stranger for her own sense of propriety.

Her job was to nurse the man back to health and set him on his way, nothing more. But her fingers still tingled from her touch against his sun-kissed skin. She realized as she lay in the dark that she held them against her lips. She dropped her arm to her side and clenched her hand tight, willing her mind to veer off to another topic.

She should be focusing on how to keep Babe safe from her papa dreams. Or she could figure out how she was going to take over the claim again with the newly excavated mine and Babe more at risk than ever. Now that the child had her papa notions, she'd also be interviewing each male she met along the stream, filling him in with her innocent way on how her mama needed a husband so she could have a papa. The child could humiliate her mother without even trying. Emma tossed onto her side, trying to escape the mental picture of every man in the area applying for the job of Babe's papa.

No, she'd not go there. She needed to find a replacement for Mack. That would solve her problem of keeping Babe at home until this silly phase wore off. More than likely, Emma's nerves would wear out before that ever happened, but she could dream. Her daughter didn't have the run on fantasies.

The thought made her glance over at the curtain that separated her from the attractive stranger. Maybe she should have kept it open. She could have watched in the moonlight to be sure he was okay.

Now she lied to herself! She only wanted the curtain open so she could stare at his handsome silhouette without his knowing. If truth be told, she suddenly wanted Babe's desire for a papa to come true as much as Babe did. She'd become smitten with the dark, mysterious man.

She huffed out a sigh at her ridiculous thoughts and flipped to face the opposite way. As if her thoughts would stop just because her back now faced the curtain. She could hear his steady breathing and resented that he could sleep when her overly tired brain ran wild with foolish emotions. After a good night's sleep, she would be able to face the error of her ways better. If only sleep would come and rescue her. She sighed again, the sound louder than she'd meant it to be.

"You might try counting sheep. It always works for me when I'm restless." Josiah's voice, full of laughter, carried across the room.

He'd heard her tossing and huffing and sighing! Her face flushed so deeply she opened her eyes to see if the red radiated throughout the cabin, lighting it for all to see. The intimacy of his being so near stifled her.

"I'm sorry. I didn't mean to keep you awake." Her voice sounded loud in the dark. It had been a long time since a man's presence had filled the tiny cabin. "I'm not used to sleeping in such tight quarters."

She flinched. Now she'd drawn his thoughts to her sleeping—or nonsleeping in this case—body. Simply scandalous!

"I mean by being cramped up in this tiny bed with Babe." Even worse! Now it sounded like she was fishing for a reason to move to a bigger, less crowded bed! Why hadn't she told the men to put Josiah in Babe's smaller bed, allowing the two of them to share the larger bed? Or better yet, put him in a bed out in the barn where he'd be at the mercy of the boarders instead of her?

She knew the answer to that one. The risk of infection out there far outweighed the discomfort of having him here in her cabin. He was a man. She was a woman. Those were the facts. But they were both adults. They needed to buck up to the situation and act like it. She had to figure out a way to divert their focus away from their sleeping situation and close proximity before they said or did something immoral. She had no intention of dishonoring God through her thoughts or desires.

"Mack's responsible for my brother's death."

All right, then. Maybe only her thoughts and actions needed to refocus. Apparently Josiah's thoughts were far, far away from her prone form lying on a bed mere feet away from his own. She interrupted her own musings as his words sank into her sleep-deprived brain. "Mack killed your brother?" Surely she'd misunderstood. Or the medicine had taken effect and caused the man to talk crazy.

"Inadvertently, yes." The words came with a hesitance, as if he'd rather blame Mack for outright murder than admit an indirect action.

"How?"

"Are we going to wake Babe up with our talking?"

Josiah's consideration for her daughter touched her heart. This man, stranger or not, didn't seem the type to harm a woman and her daughter. And he felt less a stranger the more time she spent in his company.

"No, once she's out, nothing will rouse her." Emma rolled back over to face Babe and the curtain. She pushed her daughter's hair off her face. The motion didn't change the rhythm of Babe's soft breathing. "Tell me about your brother."

"We were partners with Mack, had grown up with him through our childhood years. We had no reason not to trust him." He grew silent.

Emma let him gather his thoughts.

"We worked various jobs as we traveled, headed out

West, and had amassed a small fortune. The plan was to earn enough to start a ranch that would be big enough for us all. We'd be able to buy everything we needed from the start and would work together to make it a success."

Again he paused.

"I'm listening." She didn't want him to worry that she'd finally nodded off during his painful narrative.

"One morning we woke up to find Mack gone, along with our money. We searched high and low for him over the next few months. My brother, Johnny, couldn't handle it and began drinking heavily. Next thing I knew, he'd gotten himself into a skirmish at a saloon and ended up with a bullet in his heart."

He stopped.

Emma waited, not knowing what to say. She prayed for the right words to come. "I'm so sorry." Maybe not the most profound words, but they were from the heart.

Josiah still didn't speak.

"I understand your animosity toward Mack, but why do you hold him responsible for the bullet another man used to send your brother to his death?"

"We both—my brother and I—were raised better. We both loved God and relied on our relationship with Jesus. He was a huge part of who we were."

Emma didn't miss the past-tense reference to his relationship with God.

"Johnny wasn't a drinker. Everyone loved him. His joy of life radiated out to all who knew him. He began to drink only after we'd lost our dreams, the dreams that Mack stole from us."

"Why would he do such a thing? Did you have a falling

out? Did you see signs that Mack felt slighted or angry or left out?"

"We had no warning. One night Johnny and I headed off to bed, worn out from a heavy day of work. Mack said he'd join us later, that he had things to do. We didn't either one give it another thought. The next morning, we woke up and checked his room at the hotel, and though his stuff still filled the space, he'd not slept in his bed." Josiah shifted in his bed and groaned at the effort. "Ah, I've got to remember not to lie on my left side for a few more days."

"Do you need me to get you anything?"

"No, I'm fine. I forgot for a moment about my head."

Emma figured that was a good thing. If he could forget, the pain must be lessening. "So he hadn't slept in his bed. . . . He'd already skipped town?"

"We weren't sure what had happened. Mack, though brought up the same as us, had always tested the limits. He liked to have a drink or two at the saloon, and we figured he'd struck up with a woman. The thought upset us, but when he didn't come around for a couple more days, we became alarmed. No one seemed to know where he'd gone. He'd disappeared into thin air."

"Did you track him to a saloon?"

"One man said he'd seen Mack enter the saloon, but no one seemed to have a memory of what happened to him after that. We were in the process of rounding up a search party and stopped by the bank to pull some money to fund the trip. That's when we found out we'd been had, and Mack had taken the whole lot and run off days before."

"I don't know what to say." Mack had worked around

Emma and Matthew for years. Had he robbed them right under their noses, too? Had the new mine or the claim produced gold that Mack had kept for himself? She hated to even entertain such thoughts, but now that she knew his character, the thoughts and doubts were there. "He's worked off and on with us for so long. . . . Why didn't I see it? Would he have harmed Babe and me in order to get our money if we found a fortune, too?"

Josiah released a pent-up breath. "I don't have an answer for that. I'm just glad I came along in time to prevent him from reaching his plan, whatever it might be. If that was my purpose in being here, it's a good start."

"What do you mean, 'start'? What's your plan?"

"Emma, I have to avenge my brother's death. The loss of his life can't be in vain." Josiah's flat words were cold, emotionless.

"You have to let the anger go, Josiah. If you hold on to it, you'll end up just like Mack, or worse. I saw an undercurrent of anger in him of late, enough to have me on edge before you arrived. I'd already decided I needed to let him go."

"I'm glad you didn't."

"Because you want him for yourself?"

"No, because I have no idea what he'd have done if you'd cut him off before he found his next treasure. He'd likely have harmed you or Babe."

Emma shuddered and pulled Babe into her arms. She needed to feel her daughter's heart beating against hers. Josiah's first thought had gone to her and Babe's safety. That was an improvement. A couple of days ago she'd have seen a different reaction from him, she was sure.

"My head's starting to pound again. I need to rest. But, Emma?" He stopped to make sure she still listened. His voice was starting to slur.

"Hmm?"

"Don't judge me for my actions until you've walked in my shoes."

"It's not my place to judge you, Josiah. That's between you and God. I only know that if you don't focus back on God, you might end up angry like Mack. . .or dead like your brother." The thought shouldn't bother her as much as it did. She hardly knew the man. "One more question. Where's the fortune now? Mack doesn't appear to have money. Wouldn't he have set up his ranch by now if that was his plan?"

"I'm not sure. That piece of the puzzle doesn't make sense, but I'll figure it out before this is all over."

"Do you need anything for your head? A cool cloth?"

"Nah. It's nothing a good night's sleep won't cure. I'm not sure what came over me and caused me to talk so much."

Emma's soft chuckle filled the air. The medicine had loosened his tongue. "Yes, what happened to the man too tired to speak a bit ago?"

She could hear the laughter in his responding words. "I needed that time to refocus my thoughts. I didn't think the direction they were heading was a good idea."

Again Emma felt her cheeks fill with red. But this time a certain joy accompanied her embarrassment. Josiah sounded more at peace than he had since his arrival. Maybe she'd be able to help him work through his anger toward Mack and let it go. And beside that important fact, she was relieved to know that apparently she wasn't the only one corralling her wayward thoughts after all. It would be interesting to see what the morning would bring.

seven

Emma woke early and dressed in the dark, taking extra care not to wake Babe. She'd slept in her dress from the day before, knowing she'd need to check on her patient during the night. She peeked around the curtain at Josiah, who still slept soundly, his rhythmic breathing a reassuring sound to her worried ears.

Josiah had had a rough night. Several times his thrashing had awakened her, and she'd gone to calm him, concerned that the medicine, while numbing the pain, would cause him to do damage to his stitches. The concoction apparently led to nightmares and hallucinations. Or maybe it was just Josiah's fighting his own demons that caused his lack of sleep and turmoil. Regardless, Emma hurried to his side each time and did her best to waken and calm the man, sitting by him until he fell back into another restless sleep. When he moaned in his slumber, she'd reluctantly measured out another dose of the laudanum, as the pain seemed too great for him. Now, at dawn, he finally slept in peace.

The morning light that slid through the window allowed her just enough brightness to heat the stove and prepare coffee. Quietly, she worked to make breakfast. She stirred up a pan of biscuits then set them aside. She'd heat the biscuits whenever she heard her housemates rouse and would fry up some ham and eggs to go along with them.

Pulling a warm wrap around herself, she stepped out

onto the porch to drink her coffee while having quiet time with God. She loved to sit out there and pray, taking in the beauty of the sun as it rose over the hills. No one stirred over at the barn, though usually some of the men would be up and about and would wave as they headed to the mines for an early start. Though tired, she needed this time to gather her thoughts. Once Babe awakened, she'd not have a moment to form another cohesive thought.

She lifted her cup to her mouth and froze as she heard a sound in the trees. Half standing, she worried Mack had returned. He knew her early morning routine, and it would make sense he'd try to contact her at that time, when he knew no one else was around. She knew Josiah was in no condition to help her in a crisis, and she doubted any of the snoring men in the closed-up barn would come to her aid.

Having her coffee outdoors probably hadn't been the best idea for today. She should have stayed within the safety of her home, with the door latched, until the situation with Mack was resolved.

Just as she stood to hurry inside, the trees parted and her friend Liza stepped through. Emma put a hand to her heart in relief. She hadn't realized how tense she'd been until that moment.

Maybe it would still be best to move Josiah into town. But then again, moving him wouldn't guarantee her and Babe's safety in the event Mack returned with a vendetta of his own. And she couldn't ask the boarders to give up days at their claims to watch over her. She'd feel safer with Josiah here and would have to take their situation one day at a time.

"Hi, Emma. Is it too early? I know you like your quiet time, but I took a chance you'd be up for a visit."

Her good friend must have caught wind of a stranger on the premises and had to come check out the situation.

"Come on up and have a seat. I'll get you some coffee." Liza smiled with relief and sank into a chair.

Emma slipped inside and poured another cup of coffee for her friend, wondering over the visit. Maybe it had to do with Josiah, but Liza looked pale and didn't seem her normal bubbly self. Though how else would she look this early in the morning, before she'd even had a chance to make herself a cup of coffee? She exited the door and closed it gently behind her.

Liza stared into the distance, not appearing to notice the sunrise as it burst into color before her.

"Liza? Everything okay?" Emma spoke softly, but Liza still jumped at the sound of her voice.

"Oh. Yes. Well, to be honest, no." Her smile quivered, then failed. "Oh, Emma, I think Peter's going to leave." Her voice broke, and she fell silent.

"Leave? You mean, you all will pack up and move away?" Emma's heart fluttered at the thought. Though she probably had more in common with Katie and felt closer to her as a friend, Liza was the nearest neighbor, and Emma had come to rely on her nearby presence over the past two years. "What's caused this?"

Liza's eyes filled with unshed tears. "The claim isn't doing well, and we don't have the money to buy supplies. We've struggled for weeks, and Peter has grown more distant every day. I reassure him that things will be okay, but now I don't know. He came in late last night, this morning actually, and fell into bed without a word to me. I have no idea where he's been, but I could smell liquor on his breath." She set her coffee aside. "We have no money for basic food, and he manages to find himself some liquor."

Emma didn't miss the bitterness in her words. "I'm so sorry. We have plenty. I'll put together some things for you before you go."

She cut off Liza's protest before she could voice it. "You were there for me when Matthew died. I don't know how I would have made it through that time without you and Peter. Now it's my turn to give back. Let me do this."

Liza nodded.

"Where will you go if you leave? Do you have family back East?" Emma pushed away the worry that crept up at the thought. It was late in the season to try to cross the prairies. It would be a tough trip even if they left right away.

"I don't think he intends to take Petey and me along. I have a feeling he's going to bolt on his own."

"Oh, Liza, surely not. Peter has been a rock ever since I've known him. I can't imagine his doing such a thing! He loves you both dearly."

Liza sipped her coffee and shook her head. "Not anymore. He's not said two words to me in weeks. He comes in late and leaves when I'm busy doing something else so he doesn't have to speak to me. Something's not right." She set the coffee down and walked to the porch rail, peering up at the sky. "I've prayed that God would send me an answer or allow Peter to find something, anything, at the claim to encourage him to go on. But there's been nothing. I feel so empty and alone."

"I've been right here. You know you can come to me

whenever you need to. Why did you wait? You shouldn't carry this burden alone."

Liza glanced over at her with a sardonic smile. "Did you come to us when you were struggling after Matthew passed on?" She shook her head. "No. We didn't find out until we came to visit and found the place in complete disarray. If I remember right, one of your men had to come over to ask for our help in rousing you out of the cabin."

Emma blushed as she remembered the awful few weeks immediately after she'd lost Matthew. Babe was a mess, the cabin untouched, and she couldn't drag up the energy to do more than plunk a few morsels of food before her daughter. Liza had come and forced her to carry on. She'd then teamed up with Katie, and the two dear friends kept a constant vigilance on Emma and forced her to move forward.

"You're right. I didn't come to you. But you know better and have no excuse not to come to me. We've been through so much together. We'll get through this, if it even happens. I've learned that God always has a purpose. Let me pray for you."

The women sat close together and prayed. Liza sobbed at Emma's caring words. As Emma finished her prayer, she hugged Liza close, joining with God to protect her friend in any way she could.

"Thanks." Liza wiped at her tears. "Peter will be so angry if he finds out why I've come. But I needed a friend, and after not sleeping all night, I figured I'd best get over here early so we could talk before you leave for the claim. How's that going for you, anyway?"

"I'm not—well, I haven't been—working the claim

for the past few weeks. I turned it over to Mack. But now he's missing, and I suppose I'll have to go back to mining myself." She considered asking Liza to watch Babe. They could work out an arrangement where she could compensate her friend by supplying food to her and Petey. She had doubts about it being a good idea, though, if Peter's moods weren't steady. She didn't need to place Babe into a possibly unsafe situation. She pushed the idea away. "The claim is doing okay. We've made enough to get by. We have plenty to share."

"Mack's missing?" Liza ignored her offer to help, and instead Emma's words seemed to pick up Liza's drooping emotions. "What happened to him?"

"A stranger appeared a couple of days ago and said he needed to talk to Mack. I asked him to wait, but he went to the claim instead. By the time I'd gathered up Babe and placed her with Ben Parson, they'd gotten into an altercation and Mack hit the stranger, Josiah Andrews, on the head with a shovel."

"Oh my. Was he okay?"

"He's fine, but Mack took off into the woods and hasn't been seen since." She stopped to warm her hands with her own cooling coffee. "For a moment when I heard you in the trees, I thought he'd returned."

"I didn't mean to startle you. I knew my time would be limited, so I took the direct route through the woods instead of crisscrossing on the paths. Sorry if I caused you to worry."

Emma smiled and took Liza's hand in her own. "You caused me no grief. I'm glad you stopped by. I needed a break. Taking care of Josiah kept me up all night, and you've helped me refocus for the day."

Liza asked, "Taking care of Josiah?"

"Yes. Mack's blow knocked Josiah unconscious, and he had a concussion. The men brought him here while Phil went for Doc. We figured Doc would take him right back to town, but Doc worried that any move would kill Josiah. His medicine caused him nightmares, and I was up with him until he calmed."

Leaning forward with a teasing gleam in her eyes, Liza whispered, "Is he easy on the eyes? Tell me about him. Maybe God dropped him here on your doorstep for a purpose."

"Liza! What am I going to do with you? The man's injured. That's my only focus."

"Surely you've had a moment to notice his looks. Is he someone you could look at for the rest of your life? If not, I'd think you'd send him out to the barn with the other men."

Emma laughed out loud and had to quickly hide her mortified chortles in order to correct her friend's wayward thoughts. "I suppose he's pretty easy on the eyes, but I didn't keep him in the cabin because he's pleasant to look at. The things you come up with sometimes."

"So if he were ugly, you wouldn't send him to the barn?"

Her lighthearted friend was back for the moment.

"Of course I wouldn't send him to the barn. Even if he were ugly, he'd need my care. That's all this is about. I'm interested in only the man's well-being."

"Well, that's sure good news for an injured man to hear, ugly or easy on the eyes."

Both women yelped at the sight of Josiah standing in the

open doorway of the cabin with a smirk on his face.

Emma's heart picked up a few beats. Even injured, Josiah looked heart-flutteringly handsome. A dark shadow covered his previously clean-shaven jaw. He'd need to take care of the stubble soon. Emma couldn't remember where she'd placed Matthew's shaving utensils, and then she couldn't believe she even considered finding them for this stranger. Besides, most likely he had his own supplies in his bag, wherever the boarders had placed it.

She tried to turn her thoughts in another direction. "How are you feeling this morning?"

Josiah shouldn't even be up on his feet yet. The fact that he leaned against the doorway for support showed his weakness.

"Better." He swayed in the doorway before resting against the wood frame once more. "I'll be up and out of your hair before you know it."

"So I see." Emma rolled her eyes. Why were men always so stubborn about admitting they weren't invincible? She glanced over at Liza, who still sat with her mouth gaping. "Liza? Liza!"

Her friend jumped. "Oh, sorry, you were saying?"

"I wasn't *saying* anything to you, but you're gaping." Emma glanced over at Josiah, who winked at her.

She realized her manners were sorely lacking. "Josiah, I'd like you to meet my friend Liza. She and her husband, Peter, live just over the other side of the hill, through the trees. They're our closest neighbors."

Stepping forward, Josiah reached for a chair and lowered himself gingerly to sit. "I'm right pleased to meet you. It's always good to meet one of *our* neighbors." He captured

Emma's eyes and held them captive before releasing them with a teasing smile.

A warm current ran through Emma at the intimacy of the statement. Again she caught herself wishing the illusion that they were a family could last. She realized—or finally admitted to herself—that she was lonely.

"I'm glad to meet you, Josiah. Emma's needed a man in her life."

"Liza! This is only temporary." This time she refused even to look over at Josiah, but his resounding laugh flowed across her. He had a nice laugh, even if it was at her expense.

Relief flooded her when Josiah turned the tables on her overly talkative friend. "Speaking of needing a man in your life, I hated to eavesdrop, but you're just outside my window. I heard what you said about your husband. Peter, right?"

An expression of pain moved across Liza's face.

"Maybe I could talk to him?" Josiah pinned Liza with his stare. "Sometimes it helps a man to have another's input. I don't mind."

Emma thought that was the sweetest thing Josiah could have said. "You'd really do that? For someone you don't know?"

Josiah moved his attention to Emma. "Of course I would. What kind of ogre do you expect me to be? I know I rode in here with a chip on my shoulder—"

"A boulder would be more like it," Emma interrupted.

"A shoulder boulder, Mama? What's that?" A sleepy-eyed Babe walked through the doorway and crawled up on Emma's lap.

Emma laughed. "A rhyme is what that is, sweetheart. How'd you sleep?"

Babe snuggled close. "Fine. I love to cuddle with you."

"And I, you. But I think I have a black eye today from your wiggles." Emma looked up to see Josiah watching the verbal exchange with a tender expression on his face.

"I don't wiggle that much," Babe said adamantly, sitting up straight with a frown. "Do I?"

"No, honey. I'm only teasing. You're a great cuddle-bear to sleep with, too."

Babe settled back. "I want to sleep like that every night. Then Papa can sleep in the other bed."

"Oh, Babe." She didn't even bother to correct the youngster's comment this time. It did no good. "Josiah—Mr. Andrews—won't be staying much longer. It isn't proper. He'll be on his way, or at least he'll move out to the barn with the other men."

"Until you get married?"

"Until he goes his own way."

Josiah cleared his throat, probably to hide his laughter. "I'll stick around awhile, baby doll, if it's okay with your mother."

Emma nodded.

"I still need to find Mack, and I want to help with the claim until we figure out another plan, since I ran your worker off. I'll move out to the barn today."

"Are you sure you're up to it? You need to keep those stitches clean."

"I'll be fine." He turned back to Liza, who'd sat silently ever since Babe came outside. "What do you say? Is there any way I can help?"

"I appreciate your offer to help, Josiah, but I can't accept it. Peter would be furious to find out I'd come over and talked about our situation." She stood. "As a matter of fact, I need to be heading back home right now. Petey will wake up soon, and I don't want him to be alone with Peter or wake him up sooner than necessary. Peter's too much of a bear lately."

"Mama? Can I go over to play with Petey today? I miss him."

"Not today. Another time."

"Soon," Liza added to the little girl. "Petey misses you, too."

"Okay."

"Scoot inside and get ready to eat. I'll be along shortly to finish breakfast." Emma shooed her daughter out of hearing.

Liza looked at Emma. "I'll let you know if we need anything. I promise."

Josiah forced himself to stand, too. "Let me get you some supplies. You can tell Peter that Emma had a surplus and blessed you with them."

Emma analyzed his words, wondering why she felt touched by his thoughtfulness in offering Liza her things instead of being offended as she had been when Mack referred to the claim as "ours."

"You sit, Josiah. I'll put something together." Emma hurried to collect a basket of food for her friend.

Liza followed her inside. They scooted aside as Babe barreled past, the child not wanting to miss a moment of Josiah's company.

Emma couldn't imagine the feeling of not being able to

provide for her little girl. "Tell him this basket is a thank-you gift for you all helping me get on my feet two years ago." She had plenty of eggs to share. She'd gather them in a moment. She continued to add a selection of basic foods that would carry Liza through for days.

Liza laughed. "You don't think he'll wonder why now? After two years?"

"You can tell him I've found my footing and am just getting my act together. It's true."

"I can see why." Liza's voice turned wistful as she looked out at Josiah, who held Babe on his lap. "Peter doesn't even give that kind of attention to his own son. That man you have out there is one sweet fellow."

"Josiah has nothing to do with my feelings. And he's not *my* man." Emma wondered how many more times she'd have to say that phrase before he left her place. She tucked a towel-wrapped supply of muffins into the overflowing basket. She kept one out and handed it to her friend. "Eat this before you fall on your face in the middle of the woods." She led the way outside through the back door and went over to collect the eggs. "I realized weeks ago how much time had passed me by and that I'd just barely been surviving. It's time for me to live again. . .and you'll feel the same way as soon as you and Peter get through this rough spot."

Liza wrapped Emma in a fierce hug. "Thanks for being my friend."

They walked around the side of the house, and Liza said good-bye. Emma offered to help carry Liza's load, but her friend waved her away. "I've kept you from your breakfast long enough. You take good care of him now, ya hear?"

Emma sent her back a playful glare and headed in to finish their breakfast.

"She seems to be a sweet lady." Josiah must have followed her inside. He held Babe's chair as she sat down before settling at the table beside her. He looked exhausted.

"She is. I can't believe Peter's acting as she said. I mean, I'm sure he is. Liza wouldn't exaggerate about something that serious." She tucked the biscuits into the oven and added a bit more wood to the fire.

"Failing to take care of a loved one is a huge burden for a man to carry."

Emma wondered if he referred to himself with the words. In his mind he thought he'd failed his brother. "You were sweet to offer them food."

"At your expense?" His voice held amusement. "Do you often let others give away what is yours?"

"I'd already planned on preparing a basket."

"Let me pay you back for all that you gave her. I can replace what is needed next time we go to town."

There it was again, his use of "we." Though she was sure he didn't mean anything by it, she couldn't help the smile that took over her face. A trip to town had never sounded so inviting.

eight

Josiah collapsed as soon as breakfast was over and slept most of the day away. He woke up in time for dinner, ate ravenously, and then fell back into bed again.

Emma kept Babe entertained outdoors as long as possible then brought her in for bed.

"I don't wanna go to bed," Babe whined. "It's barely dark outside. I want to play with my papa."

"For the hundredth time, he isn't your papa." Emma didn't think her patience would last until Babe crawled under the covers. The child had been irritable all day, and Emma hadn't slept well the previous night. She wanted nothing more than to settle Babe in and to give in to the weariness that consumed her body. "Hold still while I get your gown over your head."

Babe continued to wiggle and whine.

Emma captured her with an arm and held her steady while slipping the white nightdress over the small child's body. Babe felt a bit warm. Emma hoped she wasn't coming down with something. It would be bad enough to care for Babe when low on sleep already, but even worse for Josiah to catch something in his weakened state.

Babe began to cry. Emma pulled her onto her lap and sang to her softly. The child lay stiff in her arms, but exhaustion soon won out, and she relaxed and fell into a deep sleep. Emma eased her onto the bed and pulled up the bedclothes to tuck her in.

She checked on Josiah, saw that he was sleeping soundly, and turned down the lantern before climbing into bed next to Babe. She said her prayers quietly but didn't get far before dropping off into a deep sleep herself within minutes.

æ

The next morning, Josiah woke up before Emma and Babe did. He felt much better, so he crept out of bed, careful not to wake them. He eased the door open and slipped outside into the early morning air.

Everything felt fresh up here in the hills, and Josiah relished not having to breathe in the dust that had been his companion on the trail for far too long. The aroma of coffee brewing carried across the yard, and Josiah followed the enticing scent to the barn. He needed to check out his new quarters anyway. He felt good enough today that he might as well make the move. Now would be a good time to speak to the men and settle in. They'd be heading to their claims soon.

A booming voice carried through the pre-dawn dim. "Hey, it's the knockout man. Come on in and get a cup of coffee."

Leaving the barn doors open as he'd found them, Josiah let his eyes adjust to the lack of light and followed the voice.

"Phil Duggin," a younger man greeted him. "Have a seat. We're glad to see you up and around. We weren't sure for a while there whether you'd come through or not. That was one nasty bump to the head."

Josiah nodded as he sipped the warm coffee Phil placed

in his hands. "Josiah Andrews. Glad to meet you." He shook Phil's hand and looked around. The structure was sparse but more like a boardinghouse than a barn, from what he could see. He turned his attention back to Phil. "Were you there when the. . .accident happened?"

"Not much of an accident from what I saw, but yes, I was one of the men who helped. I went for Doc. I grabbed my stuff while in town and moved out here myself the other night. Emma said she had room, and I like the location."

"You have room for one more? I'd like to get out of Emma's hair now that I'm up and around. She's been good to me, but she and the little tyke seemed to be faring poorly last night and this morning. I'm thinking she isn't getting much sleep with me around."

Phil motioned for Josiah to follow him. "Most of the men went on up into the hills already, but I'll show you around. It's a nice arrangement. I took over Mack's area. We stored his things up front so he can pick them up whenever he returns." Phil motioned to a stack of belongings in the far corner by the door. "I know the men said they had another spot in the back here. Let me show you."

The area was clean, private, and welcoming. It had a cot, a small table and chair, and a shelf for clothes.

"The first men that boarded with the Delaneys took the liberty of closing the back area off into private rooms. The space above your room can be used as storage if you need it. Most of us live pretty sparsely, though, and are fine with just the room."

Josiah thanked him and decided to move in as soon as Emma woke up. His horse already occupied a stall at the front of the barn, and he walked over to check on him.

"Pretty comfy there, eh, fella?" He greeted his stallion with a pat to the head. From the looks of things, he'd never get Rocky out of here again. His mount was so well fed and gleaming with attention, Josiah knew he needed to thank whoever had cared for the creature.

He headed back to see if Emma was awake. No sign of life came from the house, so he settled on the front porch, exhausted from the effort of exploring his new home.

❧

Emma awakened, shocked to see the late hour. She and Babe never slept this late! But then, they'd never had a houseguest who needed such care, either. Josiah! She'd slept so hard she hadn't checked on him once. When she found his bed empty, she stepped outside to see him sleeping in a chair on the porch. She slipped back inside and made coffee, biscuits, and eggs. Babe slept through all the banging of pans and slamming of the stove door.

The food was ready before her daughter and houseguest roused enough to come to the table. As Josiah sat down, Emma noticed that he still looked exhausted. She knew Doc would be back soon to check on him. He'd first said he'd return today, but the miners had told her the previous night that Doc had been called out the other direction, and it would be another day or two before he returned to the cabin.

"Do you need anything? Something for the pain? You're pale." Emma stated the obvious, but Josiah might not know how rough he looked.

"No, I'm fine. I went out to explore the barn, though, and I think I'll move my things over today and stay there from now on." He poured Emma a cup of coffee before filling his own mug. "I'll be fine as soon as I'm settled. I'll rest a bit as soon as I have everything in place."

Emma eyed her food but didn't feel like eating. She picked at her biscuit while they talked. "Are you sure you're ready? Maybe it would be best to wait until Doc takes a peek at you."

"I've met Phil Duggin. He seems like a good man. He told me he'd help with anything I need, so I think I'll be fine. The men can always come for you if I need attention."

"Sounds like a good idea. But do send someone to call for me, no matter the hour, if there's anything at all that you need."

"Will do." He pushed back in his chair. "Baby doll? You want to help me carry my things outside?"

When Babe halfheartedly nodded her head yes, Emma knew something was up. She watched as her little girl slid off her seat, her food barely touched. "You feelin' all right, Babe?" She reached over to feel Babe's forehead.

"Yes, Mama. I'm just tired."

How she could be tired after sleeping so hard the night before and so late that morning was beyond Emma's understanding, but with Josiah's arrival, the little girl had been surrounded by excitement. Maybe with Josiah in the barn, they'd both catch up on sleep that night.

&

Emma had a lot of chores to do over the next two days. She washed their clothes and bedclothes, baked bread, tidied up the cabin, and fell into bed exhausted both nights.

Josiah kept insisting that he should go to the claim, but Emma assured him the claim would be fine for a few more days without their attention. She had wanted Doc to give Josiah a clean bill of health before he began his work. Instead, the stubborn man had worked around the cabin, clearing out weeds that had taken over during Emma's lack of attention while working the claim, shoring up the fence where it had sagged, and mucking out the stalls while the other men were gone. Though the miners did a lot around the place to show their appreciation to Emma for letting them stay there, knowing she didn't have a man around to keep the place up, there were still things that they never had time to do. It was nice to have Josiah taking over those chores, though Emma was sure he'd have been better rested at the claim when all was said and done.

On the fifth day after Josiah's arrival, Emma forced her way out of bed with a pounding headache. Relieved to have things clean and some food made in advance, she promised herself to take it easy. She'd overdone things while caring for Josiah and now would pay the price.

Babe continued to be cranky, and this morning she didn't budge when Emma tried to wake her up. She decided to let the little girl sleep, hoping the extra rest would improve her mood.

Emma went outside for her usual quiet time. After praying, she watched as Josiah approached from the barn. They'd gotten in the habit of sharing coffee and breakfast each day, her way of thanking him for the work he'd done around the place. "Doc should be here today to check you over. From the look of things, I'd say he'll declare you well enough to do whatever you want."

Josiah sent her a smile. "So you're saying I'm looking good? 'Pleasing to the eye,' as Liza would say?"

Emma's face heated at the comment. "You didn't miss

a thing from that conversation, did you? How do you know you didn't imagine those words while you had your concussion?"

"If I had any doubt, your blush a moment ago proved otherwise." He settled in his chair and laughed. She'd placed his coffee on the rail, and he reached for it and took a sip. "Ah. This hits the spot. It's been a mite chilly the past few mornings."

"Do you have any blankets? The barn can get quite cold. We have extras if you want some."

Josiah surveyed the clouds. Gray and fluffy, they promised rain. "I might have to take you up on them until I can get to town. I still owe you a trip. Do you feel up to going soon?"

"I'm caught up on things around here, so we can go at any time. Maybe after Doc arrives, we can go the next day?"

He nodded and drank his coffee, quiet for a few moments, lost in thought. He finally glanced around. "Where's Babe this morning? I thought she'd be up and ready to follow at my heels again today."

"She's not feeling well, but I guess I do need to rouse her. I can't let her sleep all day."

"You look a bit pale yourself. Let me get her, and you sit and relax. I'll bring her out here." He rose and walked into the cabin. Emma didn't have the energy to argue. She tipped her head back against the chair and let the cool breeze soothe her body.

She must have dozed, because when she opened her eyes, the sun had changed position. Babe and Josiah were nowhere to be seen. She stood to her feet and swayed, grabbing the porch rail for support. Leaning forward against it, she shaded her eyes and looked out toward the fenced area where they let the horses and cows roam—Babe's favorite spot for Josiah to take her. There was no sign of them.

Dizzy, she walked to lean against the front wall of the house, and a feeling of panic washed over her. Where was Babe? She'd trusted her with a stranger, had fallen asleep, and now her daughter was gone.

She stumbled into the house and saw Josiah sitting in the rocking chair, a sleeping Babe held safely in his arms. Relief swept through her until she noticed the look of concern on Josiah's face.

He stood, walked over, and eased Babe down onto her bed. He'd stripped her down to her last layer of clothes. "Emma, I don't want you to get overly concerned, but have you noticed Babe running a fever lately?"

Emma tried to gather her thoughts. Her woozy brain wouldn't work properly. What was wrong with her? "Um, yes. I think she's felt a bit warm a few times over the past day or two. Maybe longer. She's been irritable and not quite herself for the past three or four days." She stopped and ran her hand across her aching forehead. "I thought it might be excitement due to your arrival, but she might be taking sick. Why?"

"I don't want to alarm you, but she's burning up. I've been rubbing her down with a cool cloth, but it isn't helping much. I think I'd better ride for Doc." He closed the gap between them. "You don't look much better. I came out to get you when I couldn't rouse her, and I couldn't get you to wake up, either. I figured you were plumb worn out." He reached over to feel her forehead. His touch sent shivers through her, but her skin felt as if it were on fire.

"I'm fine. Let me check on Babe. I need to cover her up."

"No, she's burning up already. We need to cool her off, not trap the heat in. She can't afford to get any hotter."

A sob escaped Emma's throat. She couldn't lose Babe. Her little girl's flushed features and labored breathing informed her that she was very sick. She bent down and recoiled at the heat in Babe's skin. "I don't know what to do. I can't think. Yes, do go for Doc. He should be heading this way anyhow. Maybe you'll meet up with him on the way to town."

Josiah stared at her, concern written all over his face. "Emma?" His voice seemed to come from far away.

Emma tried to respond but couldn't. She turned to look at him and felt herself start to fall. Then everything went black.

nine

Josiah caught Emma mid-fall and carried her to the bed that had been his only a few days earlier. He laid her gently atop the covers and felt her fiery skin. Babe wasn't the only one sick. For the first time in his life, he felt overwhelmed. There'd never been a situation in which he didn't feel in total control, but suddenly these two females were sick and totally reliant on him. They'd been so good to take him in; he didn't want to let them down. He didn't dare leave them alone long enough to ride to town. Even Liza's or Katie's would be too far away.

He sent up a rusty prayer to God, begging for help. If someone would just stop by, Josiah could either send him on for Doc or have him stay while Josiah went himself. He was afraid if he left them now, Babe might get up and wander off in her delirium. Emma was too ill to care for her. She'd never even hear her daughter if she tried to go outside.

Babe cried out, and he hurried to her side. "Papa!"

"I'm here, baby doll. It's okay. You're going to be okay. I'll take good care of you." He pushed the damp blond hair back from her face.

She continued to sob. "I need you, Papa. I hurt. My mouth hurts."

Josiah's heart melted at her words. He carried her over to the window and angled her for a look into her mouth. He cringed at the sight of the open sores that coated the insides of her cheeks and throat. "Ah, no. Not this." He pulled the little girl close against him, opened the front door to allow cooler air to filter in, and sank back down onto the rocking chair. He gently rocked, crooning sweet words to the helpless little girl in his arms. If his suspicions were correct, the little girl had smallpox. He reached over to the tepid water in the bowl beside him and resumed rubbing her down with the cool cloth. He prayed like he'd never prayed before.

Hours later, he heard the arrival of someone on horseback. He tried to place Babe on her bed, but she whimpered and clung to him. He took her along to the door, relief spreading through him as he watched Doc ride up to the porch. "You're a sight for sore eyes, Doc."

Doc glanced up at him, then at Babe. "I thought I came to check on you, but it looks like I have a new patient." He tied the horse to the porch rail and grabbed his bag from the saddle.

Josiah put a hand up to stop the doctor. "If I'm correct, Doc, Babe and Emma both have smallpox. You'd best stay where you are and tell me what to do from there."

Waving him away, Doc continued up the stairs. "I've spent the better part of each day since I've seen you caring for folks just like these two. After years of treating patients with the disease, I've never caught it. I'll be fine."

He entered the cabin and motioned for Josiah to lay Babe down on her bed. Josiah hovered, not wanting to stray too far from the little girl who'd stolen his heart. She looked so frail and helpless lying there. He'd do anything to get back the impish girl who talked incessantly, always full of intelligent questions.

Doc examined Babe's mouth, then lifted her gown and checked the rest of her body. "Yes. It's smallpox. I'm afraid there's not much I can recommend for you to do, other than keep her cool and calm." He looked over at Emma, who tossed and turned on her bed. "Looks like her mama is in the same boat."

He walked over and pulled the curtain closed while Josiah returned to the rocking chair with Babe. The skin on his arms burned from the heat coming off her tiny body. Doc's silence as he checked Emma made his heart beat faster. He wished he could go over and see for himself that she was okay. He knew it would be improper, but he'd come to care deeply for her in the short time he'd stayed at their place. Emma had no one else to watch over her. The thought worried and bothered him at the same time. It wasn't his place to worry, but for the first time in years, he wanted to settle down and care for someone. He couldn't think of anyone better than this sweet lady and her daughter. They had captured his heart.

"Emma's in the same condition. I've given her something to help her sleep. I'll leave it on the table over there, and you can give her more when needed." Doc rounded the curtain. "You're going to have your hands full. I don't know what to tell you." Pulling his glasses off, he held them while he stared at Josiah. Concern etched his features. "I'd send my wife over, but she's taking care of a family on the other side of town. They're all down with the pox and have no one to care for them. At least Emma and Babe have you. You realize I'll have to place you all under quarantine?"

Josiah nodded, familiar with the routine. He'd already been exposed and sailed through the last quarantine with only a light case of smallpox. "What about the men at the barn? They've all been around me and also Babe."

"Ben Parson came down with the virus the day you came to town. I'm sure he and Babe were exposed at the same time by whoever brought the disease in." He packed his bag. "But the men here have all been exposed already. They can go ahead and work the claim or hang out here, whatever they feel up to, but I don't want them anywhere near town."

He quieted, deep in thought. "I think Liza and her clan have already had the pox, too. I'll head over that way and see if she can't come over to help."

Josiah couldn't explain the depth of relief that he felt at Doc's words. He knew the last thing Emma would want was for him to care for her in a deeply personal way. He'd hold down the fort and do whatever needed doing, but if Liza could come over to do the daily personal care, he'd be forever in her debt. Otherwise, he'd eventually have to face up to a very put-out Emma.

"Let me take a peek at you before I go. Though you look fit as a fiddle, from what I can see."

Josiah started to stand, but Doc waved him back into the chair.

"I can do what needs doing right here." He poked and prodded at Josiah's stitches and bruised head. It wasn't near as sore as it had been days earlier. "You can send up a prayer of thanks that it's healed wonderfully."

"I'll do just that. I've not prayed in years, not until today. You are an answer to my prayers, showing up like you did."

"I'm glad it worked out. Keep the ladies as cool as you can, but there isn't much more you can do. The sores will start to break open, and it's important to keep them from being infected. If Liza can help with bathing the ladies, you might wash their sheets daily so they can keep as clean as possible. It won't help that they'll be sweating through this fever. Fortunately, the fever will lift about the time the sores break open. If they get to that point, they should heal just fine."

Josiah's heart sank with worry. He knew the doctor's words were meant to encourage, but he also knew smallpox was a deadly disease and played no favorites. The next few days would be critical to whether Babe and Emma pulled through. Only time would tell if they both would make it.

❧

"I think she's coming around. Josiah, come over here and tell me what you think. The fever seems to have broken."

Emma struggled to place the familiar voice. The darkness dragged her back, but she fought it. Liza. The woman speaking had to be Liza. But why was she here, and why couldn't Emma open her eyes?

A strong hand covered her forehead. "Thank God. You're right." A laugh rang out over her head, causing Emma to jump.

"Josiah! Shhh. You startled her."

"Oops, sorry."

The hand moved away, and Emma felt a loss. A cool cloth replaced his touch.

"If you'll step outside and bring in those fresh sheets, I'll bathe her and she'll feel so much better. The worst is over. Now we just have to keep the sores clean so they don't get infected."

Josiah's voice murmured his agreement, and Emma heard

a door open, then close.

"Em? Can you hear me?" Liza caressed her with the cloth. "You've been unconscious with a fever for days. Smallpox. Babe's here and doing fine. Josiah's taken excellent care of you both, not leaving your sides unless I shooed him out."

Emma struggled to wake up. "Babe." Her voice croaked, but Liza apparently understood.

"Oh, honey! Babe's here. I'm glad you're okay. We've been so worried!"

Emma heard the cloth being dipped in water, and then Liza wrung it out before wiping down her arms.

"Babe's right behind me in her bed, sleeping like the angel she is. We've already cleaned her up and changed her into a dry gown. She's fine. Her fever broke last night."

Emma opened her eyes and stared at her friend. The low level of light told her it was evening. Though a lantern burned on the mantel, Liza had pulled the curtain.

"Let's get this soiled nightdress off and get you into a fresh one. You've sweated through so many outfits during the past few days. Josiah has kept up the cleaning, cooking, and laundry. He's an amazing man."

Emma had no energy to help Liza remove the damp gown. It was all she could do to focus on her friend's words. Josiah had done all that for them?

"You just lie still. I can do this." Liza worked the garment up over Emma's torso and out from under her.

Emma heard the door open and Josiah's strong voice call into the room.

Liza called for him to wait. "I'm changing her now. Leave the bedclothes on the table, and I'll call for you when we're finished."

Emma flushed with embarrassment. She felt as helpless as a child. "Let me. . ."

No more words would come out. Too weak to talk, she knew she'd never be able to dress herself.

"Nonsense. I've done this for days." Liza stood, walked around the curtain, and crossed over to the table. Emma could hear her rustling the fresh sheets. "I've folded them just right. If we can ease you up, I'll peel away the dirty sheets and put the clean ones back in place all in one swoop."

Nodding, Emma tried to help. She felt as if all her muscles had locked up on her. Liza, small though she was, managed to do the job on her own. Emma rolled over onto the crisp, sun-dried sheet, inhaling the scent of fresh air.

"Josiah?" Emma's voiced cracked again. "Josiah cared for us?"

Liza hurried over to fill her glass with water. Emma had a vague recollection of Josiah doing the same thing throughout the past few days. She took a gulp and choked.

"Slow down now. You need to take it easy." Liza held Emma's weak neck and head up while she drank, then lowered her to the pillow. "Josiah has been a rock. We've both had smallpox already, but I couldn't leave Petey alone. I've come over each day to bathe you, but Josiah had the brunt of the work on his shoulders. You are very blessed to have his devotion. He's a special man, Emma."

Emma nodded her head. Sleep descended upon her, but she forced herself to acknowledge the thought that she'd been at Josiah's mercy for the last few days. She had no idea what she'd uttered in her fevered state or how her sick body had betrayed her.

Even while married to Matthew, she'd never been this sick. Yet a stranger ended up being around to care for her in this weakened condition. The man she'd rescued from near death and a concussion had taken over the care of her and Babe. Most likely, he'd saved their lives.

She only hoped she could look him in the eye when the illness passed. Who knew what liberties he'd taken when she was at her worst? She chastised herself for the thought. She'd never seen him act as anything but a gentleman. Liza was right. He had to be a special man to stay and care for two sick females. Females he barely knew.

Babe had also been right. Only God could have sent this man to their doorstep at a time when they'd need his care the most.

Emma heard Josiah knock, and Liza called him in. Emma feigned sleep, not ready to face him. She heard him walk to her bedside and stop.

"How's she doing, Liza? Did she pull through the worst?" The level of concern in his voice surprised her.

Matthew had been a wonderful husband, but the few times she'd been ill—and when she was with child with Babe, when her mother helped her—he'd stayed as far away as possible.

She'd never known a man like Josiah, who would be so gentle at a bedside, especially when he barely knew her. It had to be his way of repaying the debt he felt he owed her for her kindness while he had the concussion. That would explain the devotion.

"She's going to be fine, Josiah. You can stop worrying now. Keep her calm and rested." She laughed. "If I know my friend, you'll have your hands full with that. She and

Babe will keep you on your toes now that they're feeling better. They won't take to being stuck in bed while these sores heal, I can promise you that."

Josiah's voice sounded choked when he spoke his next words. "If I have to tie them down, I'll keep them calm. I'm just glad they pulled through. I never want to go through days like that again. Ever." His voice shuddered. "Whew. Those were some rough days they took us through, huh?"

"Yes."

Emma heard nothing but silence for a few moments. She fought sleep, knowing she shouldn't eavesdrop but wanting to learn more of Josiah's feelings toward her.

Liza spoke again. "You've come to care for them quite deeply, haven't you?"

"I have. Babe worked her way into my heart the day I rode onto their place. Emma came out, rifle in hand, and more than ready to use it. She has spunk. I like that."

"That spunk is what's carried her through the past few days. And her daughter's a miniature of her mama."

Emma heard her friend as she gathered up her things.

"I'm off to check on Petey. Katie took him for the day, but I don't want to wear out our welcome. You take good care of these two."

"You know I will, Liza. Thanks. For everything."

Emma heard him walk over to the stove.

"I have soup ready. Take some home with you, along with this corn bread."

Emma wiped at a tear. The man cooked, too? Of course, he'd lived alone, so it made sense, but most men would stick to the basics and would never think of cooking for a neighbor like Josiah just had.

She fought off the thought that he might be after her claim and gold, too. But really. . .how was she to know that he was any different than Mack? Just on his word, the word of a stranger? Granted, Mack had never taken care of her and Babe in this way. According to Liza, Josiah had gone beyond measure to make sure both women were provided for. And he'd never shown the anger Mack kept hidden away behind his eyes, ready to come out on a whim. The men were cut from different cloth, and it wasn't hard to see which one came out woven with the richest, most vibrant depths. Josiah had quality.

He closed the door behind Liza and headed Emma's way.

She closed her eyes again and forced herself to breathe evenly. She wasn't ready to face this man who continued to take her by surprise. She'd have to face him soon enough. In her present state, she'd probably do something crazy like throw herself into his arms and beg him to marry her. Babe's imagination and dreams were rubbing off on her. She needed to wait to face him with a clearer head. It was bad enough that she had very little recollection of the past few days. She refused to do anything to embarrass herself further.

ten

"It's good to see you awake." Josiah's voice greeted Emma before she even realized she'd opened her eyes. He sat in a hard chair, which was tipped back against the wall. When their eyes met, he let the chair plop to the floor and leaned forward to appraise her, hands folded across his knees.

Emma didn't know what to do. She wanted the man to be anywhere but here. Her hair tumbled into her face in disarray, and she knew she looked a mess. Her next thought was one of wonder that she even cared what this man thought about her. But in her heart she knew she did. "What day is it?"

"Sunday." He stared but didn't say anything more.

Her befuddled mind tried to grasp the time passage. "So I've been asleep. . ."

"This fever hit four days ago."

"I've missed four days?"

She watched as Josiah winced. "Actually, that was the second phase of fever, when you broke out in the rash. See, the bumps are scabbing over now."

Emma raised her hand and saw the ugly red spots. "When did I talk to Liza?" She fought back a sob. She hated feeling out of control. "I thought I talked with her yesterday."

"Your fever broke that day, but then the rash started in full force, and you weren't yourself again all week."

The sob worked its way free. Josiah leaned forward and pulled her close. She fought to push him away. "Don't. I look awful. I'm such a mess."

He continued to hold her. "I've seen you in this condition for the past week and a half. Don't you think I'd have run by now if I were going to? There's nothing wrong with accepting help when you need it."

His arms felt wonderful around her, comforting and strong. She hadn't felt this safe and loved since Matthew died. She sobbed into his shirt until she gained control of her emotions. It wasn't right for him to hold her this way. She reluctantly pushed him away again, gently this time. "I'm okay now. Thank you."

"You aren't used to being taken care of, are you?" Josiah moved his chair back a bit, giving her space, but only a few inches. "It's time you let someone else help carry the load."

She wrapped her arms around herself and nodded, not sure which part she agreed with. She wanted a bath but felt too embarrassed to ask him to prepare it for her. "Will Liza come today?" If so, she could have her help with the bathing, and they could shoo Josiah out of the way. A sudden thought came to her. Where was her daughter? She jerked upright with a yell. "Babe!"

Josiah jumped at her raised voice. "She's fine, Emma. Relax. She's outside with Phil, feeding the animals. And yes, Liza will be over in a bit. She's come over every day to care for you." He put his hand up against his chest. "You just took two years off my life. I don't need that with the ones you already took with this illness. I've been worried sick about both you and Babe."

Emma lay back against her pillow, the sudden movement

taking out of her what little strength she'd mustered. "Sorry. I just noticed she wasn't in her bed. How'd she bounce back so much quicker than I did?"

"You know how children are." Josiah's voice was teasing, but admiration filled his eyes. "And I know how Babe's mama is. I'd assume that you were already ill when you overdid it on the cleaning after caring for me. So you went into this already exhausted, where little Babe had all her energy to focus on getting well."

Chastised, Emma ignored his comment.

"Hit a nerve, did I?" Josiah wasn't giving up.

"I might have felt a bit under the weather, but I had no clue I was about to be hit with something so serious. Next time I have a deadly illness, I'll make sure to take a couple of days off to rest beforehand."

Josiah's warm laughter filled the room. "Ah, she's back with snappy attitude and all." He stood. "I'm glad you're feeling better. If you don't mind, I'll go rustle up your daughter and let her say hello. I've been fighting her off for two days. She's bound and determined to take over my duties as your caretaker."

Emma flushed, the sensation crawling up her neck. "I sure appreciate your caring for us. Most men wouldn't have stuck around, let alone taken over in this way."

"You were too sick to care for yourself, let alone your daughter. I did what I had to do." He wouldn't look her in the eye.

"So you're saying you did this because you had no choice. . .no one else could fill the shoes? You were stuck with the job?" Emma's words showed her hurt, though she knew she had no right to feel that way. At least he was honest about his intentions.

"No." Josiah's voice went soft. "I had no choice because my heart wouldn't let me walk away from you, either of you." He reached out to caress her cheek. "Your little girl isn't the only one that's holding my heart hostage." With that comment he walked out the door.

Emma didn't know what to say anyhow. It wasn't like her to be at a loss for words, and he'd stumped her twice in the past thirty minutes. She heard his bellowing voice call out that a certain someone had asked about Babe.

"Was it Petey?" Babe called back.

Josiah's chuckle carried through the window. "No. Petey's not here."

"Jimmy?"

Babe had to know neither friend was here at the cabin. She had to be toying with Josiah. Emma smiled at her daughter's precociousness.

"Then who?" Babe sounded genuinely at a loss, as if she had run out of choices.

"How about your mama? But maybe you're too busy playing to talk to her right now."

"Noooo!" Babe's happy squeal wound around Emma's heart. Her baby had missed her. And she missed her baby.

The door burst open, and Babe flew through the room and plastered herself against her mother. "They wouldn't let me hug you or anything, Mama! Josiah wanted you all for himself. I got mad at him."

"Angry."

"Yes, that. He wouldn't let me touch you. He did all the touching."

Josiah had rounded the door and stood frozen in place,

his face burning red. "It wasn't quite like that, I assure you."

"Did you let me wipe her face down when her fever shot up?"

"Well, no. But I didn't want you to spill water on her gown and cause a chill."

"Did you let me feed her soup or sips of water?"

"No, Babe, you know I didn't. But you tried that one time—and you did a fantastic job—but remember the soup slopped, and we had to have Liza change her clothes and the whole bed."

Emma felt like a newborn babe. There she lay like a lump while her daughter and the man she loved coddled her like an infant. *The man I love?* Where had that thought come from?

"Hello, I'm right here." Emma interrupted her own thoughts, as she was uncomfortable with the direction they were heading. "Tell me what you've been doing."

Babe's eyes lit up. "I've been helping Mr. Duggin work outside. *He* lets me help." Her young eyes sent daggers at Josiah.

Emma tried unsuccessfully to hide a grin. The corner of Josiah's mouth rose into a smirk as he shrugged. Maybe the days of Babe's papa hunt were over.

"Mama?" Babe leaned against the bed. The tiny pink rosebuds on her powder blue dress accented her pink cheeks. "Do you really love my new papa? You told Josiah that while he cared for you."

Emma's blush turned to a full-fledged burn. *Scorch* might be more like it. "I didn't."

Josiah had the gall to laugh. "You did. But I knew you were delirious. It's okay."

"No, it's not okay! I can't believe I'd say something like that."

"You did, Mommy." Babe looked angelic with her chin propped upon her hands.

"Thanks," Emma muttered, wondering why on earth she'd had Josiah call her daughter inside.

"You're welcome."

Emma mentally rolled her eyes. She turned to Josiah, who was suddenly busy in the kitchen. "So what exactly did I say?"

Babe began to dance around the room, twirling her skirt, and called out in a singsong chant, "You said you *loved* him and that you'd *marry* him and that no one else has ever *cared* for you like *he* does."

Emma pulled the cover over her head.

Josiah's voice still held traces of laughter as he spoke to her daughter. "Babe, why don't you go outside and finish up with Mr. Duggin, then we'll see about getting your mama to the table to eat with us."

"Okay." Babe ran to Emma's side. She pulled at the cover, but Emma held it tightly in place. "Are you playing hide-and-seek?"

"Just the hiding part."

"Oh. That's not fun. You have to seek to make it work right. I guess I will go back outside. Maybe Mr. Duggin will play the game with me properly."

She scurried to the door after a random peck on Emma's head. The door slammed shut, and Emma thought about praying for the fever to return and take her away into oblivion. She lay quietly, hoping Josiah would stay outside after seeing Babe safely to Phil and give her some peace.

No such luck. Josiah entered and walked over to pull the quilt from her face. "You don't have to hide from me. Ever."

She blinked at the sudden onslaught of light. "Oh yes, I do."

"Look. People say all kinds of things when they're ill. I understand that. I didn't take offense. I actually kind of liked hearing it."

Emma groaned. "When did you say Liza would be here?"

"I think I hear her now." He walked to the door and called out, "You have a friend here who needs rescuing."

Never had Emma been so happy to hear Liza arrive. After Josiah excused himself to go out to the barn for the washtub, Emma sat up shakily to regard her friend. "So did I make any odd or offensive statements to you?"

"Babe told you that you declared your undying love to Josiah, huh?"

"My undying love?" Emma swayed. "No, she just said I told him I loved him and would marry him. How bad is it? You can tell me. What else did I say?"

Liza dropped down onto the bed to sit beside Emma. "He knew you were talking crazy. It's all right."

Josiah returned with the tub and began to fill it with the hot water he had boiling on the stove top. "You'll feel a lot better after a soak and fresh clothes. I'll take Babe off Phil's hands for a while and let you ladies catch up." He hesitated. "Do you mind if I take her up to the claim with me? Lunch can wait."

"No, I don't mind. Take your time."

"Good. I want to check things out. I ran up there once while Liza stayed with you both, and Phil's been watching things, but now that you're on the mend, I'd like to take a more thorough look myself." He brought over more water and placed the pan on the table. "Babe can use the change of scenery, but I'll carry her most of the way so she doesn't get too tired. We'll be back in time to eat."

Emma looked at Liza for confirmation of the plans. She hadn't considered her daughter's frailty and recent illness.

"They'll both be fine. You can trust Josiah fully with her, and she's fit as a fiddle and does need to get away for a bit. It will do her good."

"Are you still interested in helping with the claim? At least until I get back on my feet?" Emma couldn't imagine that Josiah didn't want to get on with his own life and be on his way.

"Absolutely. I told you I feel responsible for chasing Mack off. I intend to see this through."

"For how long?" Emma knew she couldn't count on him to run things indefinitely. He had a life. Somewhere. She still knew next to nothing about him. But she'd remedy that as soon as she recuperated. She couldn't trust the mine to another man who might be as untrustworthy as Mack had turned out to be. But evidence of Josiah's goodness surrounded her. Surely he wouldn't go through all this just to win her over so he could steal from her. Though it seemed clear Mack had.

"As long as it takes." He knelt down to look into her eyes. "I know things have been crazy ever since I rode up. I'm sorry for that. But I'm not sorry I ran Mack off. I'm still sure he planned to take the claim away from you. And if he couldn't, he'd just take what he found."

Emma shook her head. "I still can't believe—"

Josiah interrupted her. "Did he ask for your hand in marriage?"

"Well, yes. I told you that."

"If he married you, the claim would become his. Didn't you say he looked angry at your rejection? Why would he feel that way unless you were keeping him from what he wanted to take as his own? And I don't mean you as a wife."

His observation did nothing for her self-esteem. Emma realized he clutched her hand with his own. She liked the sensation.

"If he truly loved you and wanted to make you his wife, he would have looked hurt when you said no, not angry."

Emma had to admit he made sense. Again she shivered with foreboding. She didn't want any more run-ins with Mack, on Josiah's behalf or her own.

eleven

A week later, Emma felt enough like herself to resume her full responsibilities. She noticed supplies were running low. They'd need to take that trip to town soon. She picked up where she'd left off with preparing Josiah's breakfast before he headed out to work each day.

"Smells wonderful in here as usual," he said as he entered the house and hung his hat near the door.

Babe sat in her chair at the table and grinned up at him. She'd made her peace with Josiah, forgetting her anger as soon as he handed her the small wooden doll he'd carved for her from a tree branch. Though it was primitive, she coddled the "baby" in small blankets Emma had sewn for her from scraps of fabric.

Emma hurried to finish breakfast preparations. "I only have to get the biscuits out and we can eat."

"I see Gabby's awake and ready for her breakfast." Josiah nodded at the doll that lay beside Babe's arm.

"Silly, Gabby doesn't eat here with us. She can only have bottles. She's taking a nap. She just likes to lie by me when she sleeps." The doll hadn't left Babe's side since she'd received it.

Emma heard Josiah's chair creak as he sat down. "We need to go into town. Would today be too soon? We can go tomorrow if you have other things to do. I don't want to leave you here alone, and I owe you some supplies."

"We can be ready today." Emma looked forward to the end of her quarantine and the change of scenery. She'd taken short walks since her illness, but Josiah always kept her close to the house, not wanting to see her back in bed with a relapse. She turned to her daughter. "Baby, we're going to town!"

Babe squealed and grabbed her doll. She swung her around and danced through the room in excitement.

Emma motioned her to sit and placed the final dish on the table. "But you don't owe me anything, Josiah. I'm indebted to you for our care and can't ever repay that."

Josiah ignored her and began to dish up their food.

Emma sat beside him. They felt like a family, but Emma knew she shouldn't get attached. Even with her best effort, she'd not been able to dig out any more information about her boarder. She hadn't felt lonely in a long time, but she certainly would after Josiah headed off to other parts. His comment about her staying alone intruded into her thoughts. "Are you still worried that Mack will return and cause a problem? I'd think he would be long gone by now."

"I don't want to take any chances. He put a lot of time into his plan of trying to get your claim, from what I've seen, and I'm not sure he'll give it up that easily. We've been lying low, too, so he hasn't had much chance to act. I'd rather you both come along with me to town, so I can have peace of mind."

Emma playfully said, "I never said I didn't plan to accompany you to town. Babe and I look forward to our visit too much. You couldn't shake us if you tried."

❧

The trip into town was uneventful but beautiful. The crisp fall air filled Emma's lungs, refreshing her after the stale air at the cabin. Josiah said he had business at the general store and a few other places, so Emma and Babe decided to visit with friends before meeting up with him at a later time. They stopped by three different homes before heading over to the hotel to eat lunch.

"There's Petey and his mama!" Babe almost tore out of Emma's grip in her excitement at seeing her friend.

Emma tightened her grasp and held the child back from being run over by a fast-moving horse. "Babe! You have to be careful. That horse would have trampled you." She pressed a hand to her chest and felt her heart pound through her dress as she caught her breath.

Liza had heard the commotion and waited on the other side of the dirt road. Emma hurried across after the dust cleared. Petey and Babe grabbed each other and swung in circles.

"C'mon away from the road now," Liza prodded. "You already almost had one accident too many." She led the way up onto the boardwalk.

Though Liza's voice seemed light, her expression betrayed deeper emotions.

"Is everything all right?" Emma whispered as they reached the top of the stairs. No one else shared the area nearby. The children stood in front of the nearest window a few feet away and made faces at their reflections in the glass.

"I should be asking you the same. How are you feeling?" Liza neatly sidestepped Emma's question.

"I'm feeling fine. Great, as a matter of fact. Getting out of the house and coming to town is the best thing to happen to me lately."

Liza smirked. "Better than Josiah?"

"I'm not sure what you mean," Emma hedged. She knew her friend referred to their blooming relationship, but Emma refused to admit it. "If you mean the care he gave us, you're right. He's a very nice man."

"Right." Liza's chuckle sounded forced, maybe even a mite bitter. "He's wonderful, Emma, and you'll be crazy if you let him get away. You can't afford to let a good man like him go."

"I'm not sure I have any say in holding him or letting him go. He's his own man, and I have no idea of his plans or how long he'll be around. I know you have ideas about us, but really, there's nothing there to speak of."

"You're telling me you have no feelings for him?"

"I'd be lying if I said I didn't, and you know it. I just don't know where those feeling will lead. He's a very private man. I have no clue what he's thinking."

Liza appraised her. "I know he's as smitten with you as you are with him. I've watched over the past few weeks enough to know that. And he's not the type that would ever pick up the bottle or change on you, either. He's dependable and steadfast. Don't let him go, Emma. Promise me."

So Liza wasn't doing well after all. No wonder she'd changed the subject. "Things aren't any better with Pete?" Emma kept her voice low. She touched Liza's arm, but Liza pulled away, hugging her arms against her chest.

"Pete's left us."

Emma couldn't stop her gasp of surprise. "For how long?"

"For good. He packed his things and took off. I've not seen him in a week."

Emma's heart plunged. Some friend she was. Liza had suffered silently, alone, for a week, and Emma had been so caught up in her own world and recovery that she'd not taken a moment to wonder why Liza hadn't come around. But she knew that even if she'd analyzed Liza's absence, she'd have figured that after all the time Liza had spent at their place, she needed time to catch up on her own work. Liza's absence after her daily visits should have alerted her to the problem. Not once had Emma suggested they go over and help or check on them.

"I'm so sorry." The words were empty and inadequate, even to her own ears. "What can I do to help?"

"Nothing." Tears coursed down Liza's cheeks, and she swiped at them angrily. "I don't know what we're going to do, though. I can't make it here alone. I have no way to support us."

"Did Pete say anything when he left? Anything to help you make sense of this?"

"No. He'd been drinking more and more, and that last morning, he just got up out of bed, packed his things, and said he was done, he was leaving, and we'd better not try to follow or stop him."

Emma didn't know what to say. She couldn't imagine Matthew doing that to them. Even Josiah hadn't run out on them when they'd been sick, and he wasn't even officially responsible for their welfare. "We'll get you through this. You won't want for anything. You have my word."

Liza wiped her tears again. "You're sweet to say that."

"I mean it. I felt the same way when I lost Matthew. Babe and I have survived, and so will you." She glanced over at Babe and Petey when she said it. Liza followed her glance and looked over, too. Both children had their mouths plastered against the glass, making faces at the shopkeeper who worked within. The shopkeeper stood just opposite, leaning on his broom and smiling. "How can you not survive with that little guy to keep you going?"

"You're right." Liza laughed through her tears—a good sign. "The things that boy does to get a laugh out of me have held me together all week."

"Well, keep holding yourself together, because the worst is behind you." Emma motioned to Babe to move on along the boardwalk ahead of them and took Liza's arm in hers. "We're heading over to the hotel for lunch. Let us treat you two, and we'll come up with a plan."

Petey grabbed Babe's arm and mimicked the ladies, nearly tripping in the process. Babe fumbled for the upper hand, not wanting Petey to hold her arm. She wanted to hold his. They tussled until they almost walked into the rail outside the hotel. Petey finally knocked Gabby out of Babe's other arm, sending the little girl into tears.

Emma sent Liza on inside to get a table.

"Here, Gabby's fine," Emma consoled, dusting off the beloved doll before handing her back to Babe. She dropped to meet them both at eye level. "We're going to go inside to eat, and I want you both to be on your best behavior. Understand? No fidgeting or fighting."

They both nodded. Emma took one child in each hand and followed Liza. A lady from the saloon lounged in the hotel doorway.

"Look, Mama! That lady don't have all her clothes on, and she's outside where people can see her!" Babe's voice couldn't have blared out any louder if she'd tried.

"Don't be rude, Babe." Though it did cross her mind that if the woman had dressed herself fully, she wouldn't be confronted by a five-year-old who threw out her thoughts on a whim. Too embarrassed to meet the woman's gaze, she stepped inside the door.

"Emma! What a nice surprise!" Sarah met her at the entry to the diner and directed her over to where Liza sat beside the front window. They were at the late end of the lunch crowd, so the room only held a few other customers. Sarah followed her over to the table and helped the children sit down. "I sent a man over to your place looking for Mack a few weeks ago. Did he ever find his way out there? I've not seen him since."

"He found us."

Sarah leaned close as she filled Emma's glass with water. "He's quite an eyeful, don't you think? Did he head on out of town?"

"No, he's actually staying at Emma's now." Liza's eyes lost their sadness for a moment and twinkled as if she couldn't resist making the statement.

"In the barn. With the boarders. . ." Emma's voice trailed off. She didn't know why she sounded so defensive. Her character spoke for itself.

Babe's voice popped into the conversation. "You mean Josiah? My new papa?"

Sarah stood straight and waited expectantly, eyebrows raised.

Emma laughed. "Babe's on a papa quest. She decided God sent Josiah to be her new papa. We're still working on that." She took a sip of her water.

"Still working on making him her papa? I see." She winked at Babe before walking off as Emma sputtered. Sarah called back over her shoulder, "Let me know when you're ready to order."

"Babe! You simply have to learn to sit quietly and keep your thoughts to yourself," Emma hissed when her choking fit had passed.

"Don't be so hard on her, Emma," Liza said gently. "Maybe if I'd been more outspoken, I'd still have my husband around. Sometimes things just need to be said."

Emma ruffled Babe's hair with her hand. "But those things seem to send me into a fit of embarrassment each time she opens her mouth lately." She shook her head. "Well, let's get something ordered so we can get on with our lunch. I'm starved."

They chatted about Liza's situation as they waited for Sarah to bring their meals. Emma racked her brain trying to think of a way for her friend to raise funds. Matthew had made things easy for Emma as far as income after he passed away. They'd already had the boarders to bring in money, and Matthew had been careful with their spending and thoughtful when buying.

She took Liza's hand and bent in prayer, asking God to watch over her friend and to make a way for her to provide for herself and Petey.

Sarah returned with the food. Petey looked ready to pounce on it, while Liza again teared up. Emma wondered how long it had been since they'd had a decent meal. The aroma of roast and glazed carrots curled up to tickle Emma's nose, and she realized that for the first time since her illness, she was also famished.

Sarah leaned down to cut Babe's and Petey's food while encouraging the women to go ahead and eat. "I heard about your smallpox, Emma. How you feelin' now?"

"I'm much better, thank you. This is the first time I've been able to get out, and this town, rough though it might be, is a sight for sore eyes!" She peered out the window before turning back to her friends. The tender roast melted on her tongue. "Oh, this is so good."

Liza nodded her agreement but didn't speak. Petey and Babe chatted away in their own little world.

Sarah looked at the window, lost in thought. "The view could be better if I could find time to get new curtains up. The old ones faded to the point of looking raggedy. You know I pride myself in keeping a homey atmosphere. I couldn't stand their dreariness any longer."

Emma looked around and had to admit the room had looked much better with the windows framed by fabric. "So business must be good if you're too busy to sew."

"More than good. I can't even find time to think lately. I've hired a girl to help, but it still takes the two of us to keep things going."

A plan began to formulate in Emma's head. "Have you thought about hiring someone to make the curtains for you?"

Liza raised her head and showed interest in the conversation for the first time.

"You know how few women live in this town." Sarah scoffed. "Other than the saloon girls—and I'm not sure sewing is on their list of abilities—there aren't any seamstresses banging down my door. Even the few women that come into town lament the lack of a good dressmaker. Their husbands are striking gold, and now that they have money to spend, they don't have anyone to sew for them like they did back East."

Emma knew that one of Liza's treasures was a treadle

sewing machine. "What if I said I knew someone who could fill that order and more?"

Sarah smiled. "I'd hire her in a moment and have a long line of women behind me waiting for their turns. Do you sew?"

"No, but Liza does."

Sarah pulled up a chair and sat down next to Liza. "Really? Would you be interested in making the curtains, and maybe some dresses, too?"

Liza nodded. "I'd love to. I'll take all the business you can send my way."

Sarah looked skeptical. "Are you sure? I'm telling you, you'll have more business than you'll know how to handle."

"I'm positive."

Emma took hold of her friend's hand. God had wasted no time in answering that prayer.

Sarah glanced toward the kitchen. "Do you have time right now to go over to the mercantile with me to pick up fabric? I don't want to rush you, but I'd love to get this room back in order as soon as I can. I only have a little time before I'm needed to help with dinner."

Liza glanced down at her empty plate and then over at Petey's. He'd all but licked his clean. "I'll be ready as soon as Emma's finished."

"No, go ahead now." Emma waved her away. "Babe and I will finish up and head that way in a few minutes. We'll be right behind you."

"If you're sure." Liza's eyes had new life as she stood and, leading Petey, followed Sarah out the door.

The quest for gold had caused so much heartache for so many families. While a few were striking gold and becoming rich, many more were struggling just to put food on the table and make it through each day. Emma wondered if the cost was worth it. Her own mine had already caused greed from Mack and problems she'd never thought about.

She shook off the heavy thought and forced her mind to stay on Liza and her blessing. Emma's heart swelled. She knew God answered prayers, and though she knew her friend had been praying for help for a long time, this answered prayer felt instantaneous.

She leaned back in her chair and watched out the window while waiting for Babe to eat her last few bites. As contentment settled over her, a commotion across the street caught her attention and chased away her happy thoughts. Her heart plummeted. If she'd thought Josiah was on the up-and-up, the event unfolding outside the window now said otherwise.

twelve

The doors of the saloon across the street had burst open, and several men tumbled to the boardwalk before rolling over the edge and onto the road. Dirt puffed into the air around them as the brawl continued. Josiah burst through the door with a drawn gun and aimed it toward one of the men.

Emma saw his lips move but couldn't tell what he'd said.

The fight stopped immediately, and the men stood to walk back to the saloon. They disappeared from sight.

Emma grabbed Babe's hand and dragged her out the front door. As she reached the steps outside, a gunshot fired from inside the saloon. Her heart skipped a beat as she wondered about Josiah's safety, but then she reminded herself he was the only one she'd seen with a gun.

The doors burst open again as a man hurried onto the wood planks out front. "Somebody get Doc! A man's bleeding inside."

Another man followed him outside. "Don't bother. It's too late for him. He'll need a coffin instead."

"Then I'll get the sheriff." The man pounded away down the boardwalk at a run in his haste to bring in the law.

Again Emma's heart pounded in fear. If something had happened to Josiah, she didn't know what she'd do. She'd come to depend on him, and Babe would be devastated beyond words.

The men disappeared inside and the excitement seemed to have died down, so Emma eased closer to the building, anxious to find out what had happened. Josiah hadn't reappeared, and though she wanted to trust him, she had to wonder what he'd been doing at the saloon and why he'd had a gun.

A man, his face pale—probably from the events that had occurred inside—stepped out in front of Emma.

She caught him by the arm as he passed. "Excuse me, but could you tell me who was shot just now?"

He jumped at her touch. "Two men were fighting after having too much to drink, and a stranger intervened. The fight went on, and the men took it outside. The stranger ordered them back inside and pulled a gun, which he held on the instigator. As they entered, the drunken man pulled a gun, and a shot was fired. The man dropped dead on the spot."

Emma was glad she'd pulled Babe close against her skirt and had covered the young girl's exposed ear with her hand. "The stranger shot him?" Josiah had killed in cold blood?

"Not sure who shot him, ma'am. I only saw the stranger with the gun, and it was pointed at the dead man. But most every man in there carries a gun. Could have been any of them." He wiped at the sheen of perspiration on his forehead. "Now iffen you'll excuse me, I need to be heading home. I don't often stop off in these types of places, and I think I just had a real eye-opener on why that is. I'll be goin' home to my missus and stay there from now on." He tipped his hat and was gone.

Emma hoped he meant it. That would be one less man

likely to run out on his family. Though troubled about Josiah, Emma didn't dare enter the saloon, especially with Babe along. Surely the victim was the inebriated brawler, as the man had said, and not Josiah.

She moved up the boardwalk, stepping aside as the sheriff rushed past, her heart heavy with concern. Had Josiah just killed a man? The image of her rescuer and protector just didn't line up with the thought of Josiah as a killer.

She glanced down the alleyway between the saloon and store as she passed and caught sight of Josiah sneaking out the back door of the saloon before hurrying down the road that ran behind the buildings. Emma felt mixed emotions. Why would he sneak out just before the sheriff arrived unless he had something to hide?

※

Emma stopped by the general store and hurried over to find Liza near the bolts of cloth for sewing, obviously so engrossed in the task that she hadn't heard the commotion down the street. She hesitated to interrupt after seeing the sparkle on Liza's face as she discussed ideas with Sarah. Her friend was excited about something for the first time in months. She didn't want to take that moment away by bringing in her doubts and concerns about Josiah.

She turned back toward the door to leave when she heard Clara, the shopkeeper, enter from her quarters in the back of the store.

"Emma Delaney! Don't you dare leave here without saying hello to me first."

With a smile planted in place, Emma turned to her friend. "I'm coming back, but I have an errand I need to run first. I'd stopped by to see if Liza could keep on eye on Babe for a moment, but she's so busy I don't want to impose. I'll just take her along and we'll be back shortly. I'll visit with you then."

"Nonsense! I have Petey in the back room with me, eating a stick of candy while I work. Liza had an awful time keeping the boy near her with all the enticing items in here, so I offered to visit with him while she shopped. Let me take Babe back with me, too. I love the company of the young'uns, and you can do your errand in peace."

Emma felt relief wash over her. "If you're sure. What if you get a rush of customers?"

"John's ready to return to the front, and he can keep an eye on things out here. He just finished up his lunch. You run along now, and if it's okay with you, I'll let Babe pick out one of those peppermint sticks she's eyeing over there, and she can join us for a bit."

Emma laughed as she realized her young daughter had wandered to the candy display while they'd chatted. The child stood motionless, Gabby hanging precariously in her hand, as she perused the many glass jars of candy lined up on the counter before her. "One piece, baby doll. Clara's going to take you to the stockroom to play with Petey while you eat your candy, and I'm going to run an errand. I'll be back before you know it."

Babe nodded, her eyes never leaving the peppermint stick that Clara removed from the jar. She wrapped it in paper and passed it over to Babe. Babe waved, then turned to take Clara's offered hand, happily skipping alongside her through the connecting door of the back room.

Emma hurried to the front of the store. Liza hadn't even noticed her presence. She and Sarah were deep in discussion over the best color and fabric to hold up to the sunlight and daily wear of curtains. A couple of other customers had eased closer and now interrupted to ask about having dresses made.

Pushing the door open, Emma hurried from the shop, nearly bumping into Katie, who stood just outside. "Katie!" Emma moved forward to hug her best friend. "How are you? I've not seen you since we became sick."

Katie returned her hug. "We've been dealing with illness, too. I was so sorry not to have been more help than I was. I helped out with Petey when I could so Liza was free to focus on you. But now we're on the mend, and I hear you are, too?"

"We are. It feels so nice to be able to walk and get around. I never want to go through an illness like that again." Emma sent up another silent prayer of thanks that they'd all made it through with their lives. She knew others in the community hadn't been so blessed. She'd need to ask who else needed assistance so she could repay Josiah's and Liza's kindness by helping the others.

She took a step away. "I'd love to stay and chat, but I have to run a quick errand, and Clara's watching Babe until I return. I don't want to take advantage of her kindness."

"I understand." Katie looked disappointed. "Promise me you'll head out our way soon?"

"Most definitely. Babe and I both are hungry for a visit and to get out of the house for an afternoon. We'll see you soon."

She hurried away from the store, following Josiah's path. When he'd left the saloon, he'd been heading east.

After thirty minutes of searching, she'd had no luck

finding him. Retracing her steps, she stepped hesitantly into the alley between the saloon and store. The air was cooler there, and she shivered, feeling as if unknown eyes watched her pick her way between the trash and debris that filled the space. It would have been smarter to walk around the block to the back side of the buildings, but that would take valuable time she didn't have.

She emerged onto the back road and looked both ways. Not many people traveled back here, mostly owners and men wanting to rest their horses in the shade. Several figures sat in clusters beneath the trees beyond the road, and Emma again wondered at the practicality of wandering alone back here with a killer on the loose.

She turned in the direction that Josiah had traveled and glanced around to see where he could have gone. The livery stood off to the side, apart from the other buildings, and she wondered if he'd gone there.

"Emma," Josiah's voice called out from the far side of the rough timber building. "Over here." He patted a wooden crate beside him.

Emma slowly walked over to join him. Her apprehension mounted as she studied his face. Though not a look of evil that she'd expect a man who'd just committed murder to wear, his expression seemed haunted.

"You heard about the murder in town?"

She sank to the box he'd offered her and nodded. "I'll ask right out. Did you kill that man?" She braced herself for the answer.

He shook his head no.

She couldn't begin to describe the relief she felt. She sensed that he told the truth. "Then why did you skulk out the back door just as the sheriff arrived? That's the act of a guilty man." She pushed her hair back out of her eyes, perplexed. "What do you have to hide, Josiah?"

"I have nothing to hide." Josiah stood and paced in front of her. "I've not been completely on the up-and-up with you, though. You know I'm here to find Mack, but I was officially sent here to find another man, the one in the saloon."

"As in a hired killer?" A shiver passed through her. Would Josiah have killed if someone else hadn't killed first?

"No. I'm a U.S. Marshal. I'm here on the side of the law. The man shot down back there was wanted on many charges, murder being only one of them. I didn't come to town today with the plan to arrest him, but as I left the general store and stashed my supplies with the wagon, I saw him through the swinging doors. I couldn't miss my chance to apprehend him." Josiah kicked at a rock in exasperation. "I wanted to capture him alive. I tried to take him quietly, but he reacted with violence. A few of the guys there jumped him. He'd been causing a ruckus with several of them it seems, so they took pleasure in helping me out. As they reentered the saloon on my command, another man pulled his gun and shot my man in cold blood. The men grabbed the killer and brought him to the floor and held him down while another went for the sheriff."

"They why the disappearing act and sneaking out the back door?" Emma wanted to believe him, but his actions didn't match up.

"I have to assume the man who shot him did so to keep him quiet. Though I didn't make it public who I was or what I wanted, the victim—or criminal, to be more accurate—knew exactly who and what I represented. He was running scared. He pulled his gun on me, and that must have been enough to make his sidekick realize he posed a risk to the operation. Before I could get a shot out in self-defense, the other man shot his buddy down before the victim had a chance to think about pulling the trigger on his own gun."

Josiah's story began to make sense.

"The sheriff knows why I'm here. I wasn't skulking around to avoid him. But with part of the gang still on the loose, and at least one member in the saloon at the time of the gunfight, I couldn't take a chance on my cover being blown. Though the gunslinger knows I had a bone to pick with his friend, he doesn't know if I was there as a lawman or as an outlaw."

"So you're free to leave? Or do we have to wait until you can speak to the sheriff about all this?" Emma's enjoyment at being in town suddenly dissipated, and she wanted to get Babe and return to their cozy cabin.

"The sheriff will stop by your place later, when he has things under control over here."

Another thought occurred to Emma. It disturbed her more than she cared to admit. "You were really here as a marshal? So now that your job is done, do you have to go back to get a new assignment?"

"I'm here to see through this situation with Mack. The man I chased here was an annoyance, and now that he's out of the way, I can fully focus on protecting you and Babe. The authorities know I have other reasons for sticking around and are supportive of my capturing Mack. At least, I need to bring him in for questioning on the theft of our money."

He stared at Emma, his gaze drilling deep into her soul. "Is there anything else you need to ask? Or can we pick up where we left off and continue this conversation after we get out of here?"

Emma licked her lips, suddenly speechless. Josiah's eyes searched for understanding, and she felt her heart tug in his direction. She stood and moved closer without consciously realizing she wanted to close the gap between them.

Josiah reached for her and pulled her close.

She leaned against him for support, her cheek resting upon his chest, the stress of the day catching up with her.

His work-roughened hand reached back to grasp her head. He twisted his fingers through her hair before gently tugging on it to tip her head back, forcing her to look up at him. Lowering his head—and much to Emma's surprise— he caught her mouth with his in a gentle but very persistent kiss.

thirteen

The dizziness that swept over Emma after Josiah's kiss caused her knees to give out.

Josiah chuckled as he grasped her tightly around the waist, preventing her from sinking to the ground. Once she was steady, he pulled back, still holding her arms, and smiled. "Now that made every bit of the day's stress go away."

Emma felt dazed. She'd come out here to see if Josiah had possibly killed a man and now stood in his arms in full sight of anyone who chose to walk around the corner of the livery. At the realization, she stepped backward and pulled out of his strong embrace. Her knees buckled again, and he touched her arm to steady her.

He gave her a crooked smile and took her arm in his, suddenly a proper gentleman for the benefit of anyone who looked on. "Let's go get Babe and head home."

Emma nodded, still too shaky and surprised to speak. She liked the way he'd said that. Home. Again, as during breakfast, he acted as though they were a family and ready to go back to their place together. She shook off the thought. Though Josiah had kissed her, he hadn't declared his undying love. She didn't want her mind—or heart—to jump to inaccurate conclusions based on one kiss.

Josiah guided her in the direction of the store, his touch gentle on her arm. "I bought the basics when we first arrived in town and stashed them in the wagon. I figured we'd pick up anything I missed after I met up with you."

He recited the list of supplies he'd bought, and she nodded, sure he'd bought everything needed for now. They stepped aside to let another couple pass as the boardwalk narrowed. The breeze picked up, and Emma shivered, the thin fabric of her seafoam green dress not much protection against the cool air. Gray clouds moved across the sun and blocked its warm rays.

"You're cold. C'mere." He pulled her against him.

Emma felt her face flame at the curious glances from some of her distant neighbors. She crossed her arms against her chest to ward off more of the chill air. Because she and Josiah weren't acting inappropriately, she ignored the stares and stayed in the warmth of his arm.

Josiah seemed unaware of the stares, or maybe he just didn't care. He smiled down at her. "I'd hoped to catch you for lunch, but obviously things didn't go as I'd planned."

"That's fine. I ran into Liza and invited her to eat with Babe and me." Emma was glad to find a safe topic to discuss. "Pete left her, Josiah. I hate what the rush for riches in the hills is doing to the families around us."

That stopped Josiah in his tracks. He turned so he could look into her eyes. "He's gone? For good?" At her nod, he continued. "I can't imagine how a man can do that to his own flesh and blood. Probably an inane question, but how's she doing?"

A couple of hours ago Emma would have given him the sad version, but now, with Liza finding hope through her sewing, she answered the question on a more positive note. Josiah cared, really cared, about people. He'd be happy for their friend. "She's holding on. I left her at the general store, where Sarah was picking out fabric so Liza could sew new curtains for the restaurant. As I walked out, I heard a couple of other ladies inquiring about her services as a dressmaker, so I think she's going to do all right."

Josiah grinned. "That's the best news I've heard all day."

"Yes, but Liza's situation has made me think. Pete came here after a dream. Then he let that dream take over him, and he made it more important than his wife and his son. . . everything. I don't want to end up like that. I want to let go of the claim. It's not worth it—all the trouble it's causing, the greed people will have for what is in these mines. No amount of gold or riches is worth the pain and danger this is bringing to Babe and me."

"What Pete did to his family is wrong, but that's not the claim's fault or anything other than a result of his own choices." He caressed her arm, his touch sending a jolt of warmth through her. "But that claim you speak of belongs to Babe and to you, and Matthew wanted you both to have it. It's his legacy. I've said it before and I'll say it again, I'm here for the duration, to see this thing through, and I'm staying until I know that you and the claim are safe."

Her heart dropped at his words. They didn't sound like the thoughts of a man planning to settle down with a wife and daughter. Though he hadn't ever said he would stay, his kiss had told her differently. But then, despite what the kiss had been to her, maybe it was only a passing fancy to him. The opportunity had been there and he took it.

Emma forced a smile to her face, though her heart felt as if it were cracking into a million tiny fragments. She pushed the thoughts away and continued, hoping her voice didn't show her pain. "I know, but riches and strife just aren't worth this to me. What else do I need? I have enough money to see Babe and me through. We have the homestead and raise a lot of our own food. We're happy."

A cloud passed across his face, but she couldn't tell what caused it. Maybe it bothered him that he hadn't entered into her equation, or more than likely, it bothered him that she would let the claim go so easily.

"I hope there's one thing more that you need."

His words confused her, but she hoped he meant he did want to be a part of their lives. He stared at her another moment, searching her eyes, then tugged her around, and they continued their stroll toward the store. She did need one more thing in life to make her happiness complete. She needed him, no doubt about it. But she couldn't yet voice the words or admit that she'd fallen in love with him somewhere along the way. If she'd read him wrong... Well, she'd be cautious and enjoy their time together then take what came up the road.

They were in no hurry as they walked to retrieve Babe, and Emma was content to bask in Josiah's company. She loved the feel of his arm around her waist and the feeling of safety his embrace brought her. She and Babe were blessed to have such a man in their lives at this difficult time.

It was no coincidence, in her opinion, that Josiah had arrived when he did. Mack had made his move, and she did not know how to stop him. She owed Josiah a great deal and hoped he stuck around long enough for her to show her appreciation. How she'd do that, she didn't know, but she would think of something.

The store loomed in front of them, and Josiah held the door for Emma to walk through.

Clara glanced up with a perplexed smile. "Did you forget something? I thought you'd long left town."

Emma's heart plummeted.

"We came to collect Babe." She forced a smile, but her heart beat a hard staccato against her chest. Surely Clara hadn't forgotten she was taking care of the little girl. Or maybe Liza had taken her along to find Emma when she left. That was surely the situation.

"But she was picked up not thirty minutes after you left her here." A sudden panic filled Clara's eyes. "Liza finished with Sarah minutes after you left the store and offered to take Babe to find you, but I insisted she stay here since we were having such a good time. By the time I returned to her in the storeroom, she'd fallen asleep on a pile of blankets. Mack walked in moments later and said you'd sent him to collect her. I didn't give it another thought since he'd been in here with you on previous trips, and he's a boarder at your place and all. . ."

As Clara's voice tapered off, Emma felt her knees weaken for the second time that day, but for a very different reason. She became aware of, and thankful for, Josiah's supportive arm holding her up, because otherwise she'd have dropped to the floor in despair. "I. . .but. . .I. . .oh no." A sob burst forth, stopping her words for a moment. "Clara, I never sent Mack over here to get Babe. I haven't even seen him in weeks!" Her words stopped again as she struggled for a breath, suddenly unable to get air into her lungs.

Josiah tightened his grip on her arm and turned her to face him. "Stay calm. Take some air in. Easy now, that's it."

She gasped and felt a rush of air flow into her lungs, and she inhaled deeply.

"It's going to be okay, Emma. Don't fall apart on me now. We've got to focus on getting our girl back. Take some more deep breaths."

He kept his gaze focused on her, and his steady demeanor and comforting words encouraged her to calm herself.

"Okay now?"

"Yes."

"We don't have any time to lose." He turned back to Clara. "When did you say Mack came by? Tell us exactly what happened."

"I'm so sorry." Clara worried her apron with her hands. "It's been nearly an hour, I suppose. He walked in all friendly-like, and after chatting a moment, he said he'd been sent to collect Babe. I told him she was asleep in the back, and he said that was perfect and headed right back there and gently picked her up, taking care not to wake her." She glanced up at her husband as he walked over to join them. "I thought it odd that he appeared relieved that she'd fallen asleep, but"—she shrugged—"it didn't strike me as out of the ordinary that you'd have him collect her. I saw your wagon out front and thought you'd all meet up out there. We got busy then, so I never noticed your wagon didn't leave. I'm so sorry."

Josiah waved her apology off. "No need to feel bad now. You didn't know. Mack's been on the run for weeks, but we haven't made it public knowledge. It's a private situation, or at least it was before he pulled this latest stunt."

Though he seemed calm, Emma could feel the tension

and rigidity of his muscles through his shirt. His fingertips dug into her arm, and he only loosened his hold when she wiggled out of the tight grip.

"Sorry, Emma." He rubbed her arm where he'd clenched it then turned to the storekeepers. "We need to go after Mack. Will one of you go for the sheriff and let him know what's happened? Tell him to meet us up at Emma's claim."

He turned to her. "Will he know where it is?"

"He knows the spot. But why there?"

"I have a feeling in my gut. That's what this is all about. It makes sense to me that he'd take Babe up there as a hostage. I think he'll use her as leverage so he can take over the claim."

"But he has to know he won't get away with it!"

"He's not thinking right, so the less time he has with her the better. We need to get going."

Emma watched as his jaw set in a firm line.

He touched her cheek with the back of his hand, wiping away the lone tear. "We'll get her. Don't you worry." His hand dropped, and he hurried outside.

Emma followed. She prayed for her little girl's safety while Josiah made plans.

"We'll take the wagon as far as your place, and then I'll continue on by horse. I want you to stay inside, with the cabin locked, just in case I'm wrong. I don't want both of my ladies in Mack's clutches." The whole time Josiah talked, he worked on readying the horses for the ride. He lifted her up onto the seat of the wagon, then paused. "On second thought, you go ahead to the cabin, and I'll run over to the livery and borrow a horse. That saves time. Stop by the sheriff's office and tell him I said that you need an escort home, instead, and that someone needs to stay there with you in case Mack heads your way."

Emma shook her head in disagreement. "There's no way you're cutting me out of this, Josiah. My little girl is with that madman, and I'll not sit at my cabin, huddling in fear, while she's out there with the man she hates. Don't you see? Babe's the only one who saw through him from the start. That's why he said it was perfect that she was asleep when he picked her up. If she hadn't been, she'd have only gone kicking and screaming. He'd have never gotten out of town." Her anger turned into a sob, but she continued her rant. "But when she does wake up, she'll be madder than a wildcat, and who knows what Mack will do to silence her. I'll not be left behind when my baby girl needs me."

Josiah didn't argue. He jumped up beside her and raced the wagon down the street and over to the livery.

The harrowing ride took seconds, but to Emma it seemed an eternity. She dared not question Josiah about his plans, not wanting to distract him and possibly cause him to rethink her going along.

He jumped down before the wagon fully stopped, unfastened Rocky, and entered the structure at a run. Within seconds he returned, digging through the parcels he'd placed in the back.

Emma climbed down and stood at his heels, refusing to let him get far away in case he decided to give her the slip. Moments later Sam, the liveryman, led Rocky from the barn. Emma noticed that the horse was saddled and ready to go.

Josiah took his parcels from the wagon to the saddlebags

and stowed them there before slipping a shotgun up over his shoulder. He pulled his handgun from the holster that had been hidden beneath his jacket, the fierce-looking weapon tucked against the left side of his chest. A revolver rested on a belt that he wrapped around his waist. It hung at a low-slung angle, where he'd be able to grab it quickly if needed. He pulled the revolver from its holster, flipped it open, and looked inside before snapping it shut and returning it to its place on his hip.

"Surely all those weapons won't be necessary." The words stuck in Emma's throat, and she had to force them out. "My baby girl is up there with an apparent madman. If you go in with guns blasting, she's likely to get hurt, and not necessarily by Mack."

"We have to be ready. I have no clue what we're riding into or what Mack has planned. Babe's safety—and yours, since you insist on going along—is my utmost concern. If you stay here, I'll be able to fully concentrate on getting your daughter safely back to you. If you don't, my attention will be split and it will be harder on all of us."

"I'm not staying," she insisted. "Now, when do we get this show on the road?"

He swung up onto the saddle and reached to grasp her outstretched hand. She clutched him like the lifeline that he was, and he swung her up behind him. Sam assured them he'd look after the wagon.

Emma hugged Josiah's waist tightly, her full skirt billowing out behind them as he urged Rocky into a fast clip. Burying her face against his back, she clung to him, trying to draw strength and optimism from him and into her fearful heart.

They headed out behind the buildings and rode toward the hills.

Emma tried to figure out how her wonderful day had gone so wrong. She took comfort in the fact that the sheriff had been notified and would meet them with his deputies, but for now they were on their own, and she had no idea what Mack had planned for her daughter. A horrible thought occurred to her, and she tightened her grip around Josiah, leaning in to be heard over the horse's hooves. "What if Mack intends to take Babe just to get even and feels the best way to hurt me is by hurting her?" Her shrill voice carried on the wind as they sped toward the mine and hopefully Babe.

"Don't be thinking like that," he called back.

"How can I not? He's angry, he's unpredictable, and he's vindictive. Babe's going to be out of control when she wakes up and sees who has her. She wasn't nice to him even at the best of times. If she fights him. . ." The wind swept her voice away.

"I said don't think like that!" Josiah's tone brooked no argument.

Emma stubbornly continued. "How would he quiet her? She's so tiny. It wouldn't take much to hurt her." Her voice broke as she pictured her trusting daughter, tears pouring down her face, blond braids in disarray, as she peered up at the scary man in terror. Babe wouldn't sit by quietly. She'd scream and hit and make such a ruckus, Mack would react in fear of being heard.

Josiah urged the horse to go faster. "Just pray, Emma. Right now your prayers will do more good than any suppositions. We don't know what awaits us up there, but we do know God is bigger than the situation. Have faith that Babe's safe and that Mack's not so far gone that he'd hurt her."

He was right. She again rested her cheek against his back and thanked God for the strong man who provided strength to her weary soul. She wrapped her arms more snugly around him, placing her hands over his chest. She could feel his heartbeat, strong and steady, and flattened her fingers over the reminder that this living, breathing champion had been sent to watch over them. She felt confident he'd do everything in his power to keep them both safe. "Babe's safety comes first."

"What?"

"Babe's safety, it has to come first. You said I'd be a distraction, an added concern, but I don't want you to worry about me. I just want you to get my daughter to a safe place."

She was surprised to hear a soft chuckle escape him. "You'd be a distraction even if you weren't here. You've been nothing but a distraction to me since we met, Emma Delaney. I can't ignore my concern for you, but I promise getting Babe out of Mack's possession and into ours will be the highest priority on my mind."

She smiled. Peace descended upon her. She had complete faith in Josiah and thanked the Lord for sending him to protect her and Babe. Though she could sense his anger at Mack through the tension that permeated every muscle in his body, she knew his focus and drive centered on keeping them safe. She figured even now Josiah's thoughts were back on the best plan of action to use when they neared the claim.

His next words were unexpected—his line of thought far from where she'd expected it to be. "Of course, if you weren't pressed so tightly against my back, I could probably think a lot more clearly."

Emma felt a blush flood her face, though she silently smirked, too. She had no intention of letting go or moving a fraction farther away from the man she loved. Even though he didn't know of her emotions toward him, and even though he possibly didn't return her feelings to the same depth, she intended to draw every bit of strength from him while she could. Deep down, she also feared for his safety but refused to add those fears to the ones that already pervaded her being. Instead, she focused on the fact that his words gave her a security that he wasn't as immune to her charms as she'd feared a bit earlier.

"I'm not moving an inch, so if you want your thoughts to be focused away from me, you'd better get us up the hillside and face up to the man who holds our most valuable treasure."

"Will do," he agreed, spurring the horse even faster. "Though only to free Babe, not from any desire to pull my thoughts away from you."

A bit later, he slowed the horse and dropped from the saddle, motioning with a finger to his lips for her to remain quiet as he lifted her down. Pulling Rocky into the shadows of the trees, he tied the horse securely. He made some motions with his hand, and the animal dropped to a resting position on the ground.

Emma looked at Josiah, curious. Stepping closer, she whispered, "I've not often seen a horse lie that way. Why is he doing that?"

"In my line of work, there's a lot of gunfire," Josiah replied in a low tone. "This minimizes the chance of his getting hit. It's for the safety of both of us—his to stay alive and mine so that he can get me out of any situation alive. Now hush before you get us both killed."

Emma shuddered at that reality, knowing it now stared them in the face.

Josiah took her hand while simultaneously pulling his revolver from its holster. Holding it steady in his hand, he urged her forward. Just before they broke through to the clearing that ran along the stream, he stopped, pulling Emma close into his embrace. His rough cheek brushed against her soft skin as he leaned in close to whisper, his breath dancing against her ear. "I want you to stay here. I'll get Babe back to you as soon as I have things under control."

Emma didn't want to stay—she wanted to find Mack and scratch his eyes out at the very least—but she reluctantly nodded her agreement. Josiah needed to work, and she had to trust him to do his job well. She had no reason to doubt his ability.

He held her tightly against his chest, whispered a quiet prayer for the situation, and then pulled back to drop his lips to hers, brushing softly against them with a promise to return. He slipped off into the trees so silently even she couldn't hear him, though she knew he had to be only a few feet away.

The sudden chill that overtook her had nothing to do with the bereft feeling she had now that Josiah's arms no longer surrounded her. Nor did it have to do with the cold breeze flowing through the treetops above her. Secure in her protected place, she'd lost track of the cold afternoon air. The chill that surrounded her held something more sinister. The air thickened, and she struggled to breathe just as she had at the store. Only this time she didn't have Josiah by her side to coax her back to a steady pace.

She rationalized that the eerie feeling had to do with only the fact that Josiah had been her rock, and now he was gone. They'd stopped running, and her focus was single-mindedly on Babe and the danger that enveloped her. But in her heart she knew her rationalization played her the fool.

She began to pray, but the feeling of oppression grew stronger by the moment. Wrapping her arms around her chest, she slowly spun in a circle and surveyed the area around her.

A grating yet familiar chuckle raised the hair at the base of her neck before she'd completed the turn. Mack stepped out of his hiding place behind a set of trees. "Well, well, well, what have we here? It appears your hero has delivered you right into my waiting arms. I have to say, the kiss was rather disheartening to watch, but the end result—your being left to my selfish devices—is surely worth the wait and tortuous display of affection."

His hair stood in disarray, his eyes darted around wildly, and—based on the foul stench of whiskey that carried over to her on the breeze—he'd had more than a little to drink. "I have to wonder what it would feel like to have you meet my kiss with such eager abandon, pressing your body close against mine, like so many times in my dreams. I'll experience that moment soon, even if I have to force the event with Babe as the dangling carrot."

Emma could only watch in fear as he stepped closer, holding his revolver with shaky hands while pointing it directly at her.

fourteen

Josiah watched from the nearby trees as Emma's expression changed from anger to revulsion, until finally, fear settled across her delicate features. Josiah had circled around as soon as he'd left Emma's side. The rustling in the trees was a dead giveaway that someone had stalked them. The unsteady drunken gait, and not-so-careful attention to noise, alerted Josiah that Mack was nearby. He hated that he'd had to use her as bait, but he was confident that he could turn things around. Only the man's reference to using Babe as bait brought him a small measure of peace. From the sound of it, Babe had been safely stashed away somewhere in case Mack needed her for bargaining power.

"You'll only know of Emma's sweet kisses over my dead body." Josiah forced his voice to sound steady, though the sight of Emma with a pistol pointed at her scared him to death. Relief passed over Emma's face. Josiah realized she'd finally noticed him standing a few feet to the left of Mack.

Josiah cringed as Mack swung the gun awkwardly from Emma to Josiah, then back to Emma again, apparently deciding he had a better chance to control the situation with the weapon focused on her. Unfortunately for Josiah, Mack was right. He wouldn't jump ahead with a gun of any type aimed at Emma, especially when the firepower was held by shaky, alcohol-directed hands.

"Lower the weapon, Mack, and we can talk this out."

"I ain't lowering anything." Mack staggered, nearly knocking Emma down as he bumped into her. He swung the gun toward Josiah, and Josiah ducked behind a tree, sure the weapon would go off in Mack's wobbly hold.

Emma reached out to steady herself against a tree, and Mack grabbed her around the waist, pulling her tight against him.

Josiah bit down an expletive. Old habits died hard. Emma now formed an effective shield for any shot Josiah could get against Mack. Since she was nearly as tall as the gaunt man, Josiah couldn't even get in a good head shot now. He silently prayed. Maybe the sheriff and his men would arrive and move in from the other direction.

He peered around the tree to see that Mack held Emma with one arm slung just under her ribs, and from the looks of it, his grip was tight enough to break them. Mack's attention was on the woman in his hold, giving Josiah a momentary advantage. He moved quietly back into the trees.

"Where's Babe? What have you done with her? I want to see my daughter." Emma's voice, now strong, carried through the greenery to where Josiah waited.

Josiah mentally applauded her. If she did it right, she'd keep Mack distracted enough for Josiah to make his move.

"Babe's fine," Mack slurred. He momentarily sounded confused. "I think. Well, if she listened to me, she'll be fine."

"Mack, where is she? She's five years old. You can't expect a child of that age to listen to much of anything, especially when she's in a situation like this. Did you leave her in an unsafe place? Take me to her, please. I'll do anything you want—just let me see my daughter."

"You'll do anything I want anyway." Mack's laugh circled around Josiah, the sound grating on his nerves.

"I'll sign the claim over to you. You don't need Babe or me. No amount of riches is worth this to me, Mack. Take me to my daughter. I'll sign the claim to you, no strings attached." The strength had drained away, and Emma's voice now held a desperate quality.

Josiah could tell she was reaching a breaking point in her panic to know where Babe was. Her next move would be to try to get away from the fiend on her own, a situation Josiah had to prevent. He had to do something, but he wasn't in place to do anything without jeopardizing Emma's safety. And Babe's unknown whereabouts complicated things. He couldn't take a chance that a wayward bullet would find its way to the small girl.

Mack laughed. "You think this is only about the claim? It's about you, *darling*. I've worked hard to prove my devotion and worthiness to you. I will have your hand in marriage before this is all done. I'll have the claim, too, but marriage to you is what I want. For years I had to watch you dote on Matthew, and now you're turning your affections toward Josiah. It's not right. I earned your love, not him."

Emma's strain carried through her attempt to calm her tone. "You don't earn someone's love, Mack. Sometimes love just happens when you least expect it."

Even through the stress, Josiah's heart leaped at her soft words, hoping they referred to him. He was nearly in place. He and Emma could hash out their relationship later. For now, he'd best focus on subduing Mack while keeping him lucid enough to tell them where Babe had been stashed.

"You'll marry me, or both Josiah and your daughter will die." Mack's comment ended in a grunt.

Emma elbowed the man at his harsh words.

Josiah got a quick glimpse of the action as he peered through the trees while moving silently around the perimeter of the clearing. His heart lunged before he ducked back out of sight. They couldn't afford to make Mack any angrier.

As Josiah stepped forward to cause a diversion, a soft sound carried across the stream from the other direction, stopping him in his tracks.

☙

Where is Josiah? Emma felt as if he'd abandoned her after he'd ducked into the trees. Was he still lurking somewhere nearby? Or had he taken this chance to go after Babe? She guessed if it was the latter, it would be for the best. Babe's safety mattered above all else, and she'd told him that. But she still couldn't help the feeling of abandonment caused by his disappearance.

Mack hadn't spoken to her since she'd elbowed him. He'd tightened his grip on her ribs and had caught her free arm in his tight clutch.

She finally spoke, wanting to keep his thoughts on her and off Babe and Josiah. "Surely you know that by hurting my daughter, you'd be hurting me. And Josiah—" She bit off the comment. She'd been about to say that he meant nothing to her, so Mack had no reason to cause the man any more pain. But she couldn't say the words that were not true. Josiah meant everything to her, and she couldn't voice the lie even to save their lives.

"What about Josiah?"

Mack's fetid breath made her gag. She tried to turn her head to the side to grab a gulp of fresh air. His hold tightened further, making Emma woozy. She couldn't catch her breath.

"Don't pull away from me. The more you fight, the tighter I'll hold you. I'll only release you when you come to your senses and agree to marry me. Let Josiah have your daughter, and we'll all live happily ever after."

"Unhand her or you'll not live at all, Mack. It's over. Give up."

Emma had never been so glad to hear a specific voice in all her life. Well, except maybe Babe's. She desperately needed to know her daughter was safe.

"In your dreams, Josiah. You'll not take another thing from me." Mack jerked her hard, turning in a circle, making them a moving target so Josiah couldn't risk a shot.

Josiah's voice carried through the trees. It was hard to figure out which direction the sound came from, even for Emma. "What have I ever taken from you, Mack? It was you who took our fortune, if you'll remember back a few years."

Mack jerked to the left. "You and Johnny always had everything going for you. You had the strong upbringing. You had the most beautiful women's attentions. You had your faith."

"We lost our parents at a young age, Mack. We never cared about the women's attentions. We had a goal to reach and worked hard to get there. We shared our faith with you and trusted you as a brother. And you stabbed us in the back for our trust and took away our dream of the ranch."

Josiah's words carried from a new direction. Emma knew he silently moved through the trees, an action that caused Mack confusion. Mack again tightened his grasp on her as he tried to pinpoint Josiah's location.

"Where is he? Where *is* he?" Mack softly mumbled. He gasped. "I know your game, Josiah! Johnny's here, too, isn't he? You're trying to confuse me, but it won't work. You're messing with my head, and I can't think real clearly right now."

He backed against a tree, dragging Emma along with him. "You're both out there, ready to shoot me. I ain't moving, and I ain't letting go of Emma. You'll have to kill us both before that happens."

Emma knew he meant it.

"Johnny's dead, Mack. I'm not playing any tricks on you with him. I never will again. You ruined him."

The pain in Josiah's voice must have struck a nerve with Mack. No one could fake the torture that filled his words. "Is he telling the truth? Tell me, Emma. You've never lied to anyone that I know of."

Emma nodded, his grip still too tight to allow her to speak. He'd moved his arm from her ribs to her neck, freeing his hand to hold his weapon toward the trees, but the act also cut off the air to Emma's throat. She pulled against his arm for all she was worth, but she couldn't budge him. His focus was single-mindedly on Josiah.

Josiah's voice, louder now, called out to them, telling Mack about Johnny's death and what had caused his demise.

"My fault? All my fault. . . I can't take any more. Enough." Mack seemed to wilt, lowering his gun, and again sobbed the word, "Enough."

Emma, aware that Mack's focus had drifted, grabbed her moment to take action.

"Can't—breathe—" She feigned a faint and went limp.

The movement caught Mack off guard as he tried to keep his hold on her, and they both toppled forward. A gunshot rang through the trees, and Emma heard a scream.

Quickly realizing the scream was her own, she clamped her mouth shut, her terror paralyzing her. She couldn't move.

A few moments later, her world went black.

≈

"There you go, easy now. Breathe deeply, that's it."

Josiah's steady voice reached through Emma's fog, pulling her out of the darkness.

"Babe."

"She's fine. I have her in a safe place. Just relax for a moment while I check you over."

Emma felt Josiah's warm hands on her head as they explored for cuts or bumps. She tried to push his hands away. "I'm fine. My baby. . ."

Josiah ignored her and continued his exploration. She liked the feel of his strong hands. They made her feel secure, as if nothing could ever hurt her again. She had to think for a moment to remember what she feared and why she needed to feel safe. . . Mack! If Josiah was with her, Mack could be sneaking off to recapture Babe!

"Mack will get her!" Emma pushed to a sitting position, her head exploding with pain as she tried to open her eyes.

Josiah gently forced her head back down onto his lap. "Shh, I'd not tell you to rest if Babe was in jeopardy. She's fine, and Mack's right here."

Emma forced her eyes open.

Mack leaned forlornly against a tree, his posture defeated, his gun missing from his hand. He seemed to have shrunk in the past weeks, now just a shell of the strong man he'd been. "I can't stand the pain anymore." Mack's voice carried across the clearing. "The guilt. . ."

Emma noticed Josiah kept an eye on the man while finishing up his examination of her. "How do you feel now? Can you tell me what hurts? Do you feel pain anywhere?"

Gingerly shaking her head, Emma eased to a sitting position. "I feel fine now. Mack held me so tightly, I couldn't catch my breath. And. . .he didn't smell very clean. Sorry." She glanced over at the hurting man. "I feel bad saying it. But between the lack of air getting to my lungs and the rancid air I did get, I guess it was a bad combination."

She took a deep breath, filling her lungs with much-appreciated air. "I felt like I was going to pass out, and I thought if I could cause a diversion, you'd have a chance to intervene. As I fell, I heard the gunshot, then felt pain, and everything went black."

"Mack went down with you. I'm not sure if you hit his pistol or if you hit that tree nearby or if you both knocked heads on the way down, but you have a nasty bump on the side of your temple. The gun went off, but the bullet went straight up in the air, so no one was hurt. If you're sure you're okay, I'll go get Babe. She's pretty shook up and scared. I don't want to leave her alone any longer than necessary."

Emma grabbed his arm, determined to go to her child and unwilling to be left behind with Mack.

Josiah didn't even bother to argue. He sent her a grin and stabilized her against the tree, holding up a finger in a motion for her to wait a moment. Walking over to Mack, Josiah ignored the troubled man's griping and tied him securely to the tree that supported him.

Mack glanced up at them with pain-filled eyes. "Enough."

fifteen

Emma waited, fidgeting, as Josiah stared down at Mack. "We'll be back in a minute. The sheriff and his men are on their way and will be here soon. Don't make things worse on yourself."

Mack nodded, dropping his head in shame. "I'm ready to make things right. I want to tell you what happened."

"Not right now. We have to get Babe. But when we return, I'll be more than happy to hear your story. Though I can't imagine what was bad enough that you felt you had to take our fortune and run."

Josiah turned and gently took Emma by the arm, turning her toward a slight path between the trees. They entered the chilly shade, and Josiah's arm circled her waist, his body heat keeping her warm. "She's just ahead." Emma hadn't missed Mack's bloody lip or black eye. She realized Josiah had wanted to kill the man for what he'd put them all through. His need to take care of her and Babe must have overruled his need to pummel the man into unconsciousness.

He hurried her through the underbrush, apparently as eager as Emma was to be assured of her daughter's safety. She had a hard time keeping up but refused to ask him to slow, and he kept his pace.

They broke through the trees, and the most beautiful sight in the world met her eyes. Rocky still lay where Josiah had instructed him to wait, with Babe curled against him on the far side. She slept like an angel without a care in the world, her chest rising and falling with each breath. A small smile tilted the corner of her mouth, as if she dreamed pleasant thoughts. Josiah had positioned her so that any stray bullet would hit his beloved horse before it hit Emma's treasure.

This was Emma's treasure in the hills, her beautiful little girl. No claim, gold, or fortune could ever replace the perfection of her daughter or her daughter's presence in her life. A sob escaped at the sight of her daughter, safe and secure while snuggled up against the horse's warmth.

"Babe."

Babe stirred. "Mama!" She jumped to her feet and ran to Emma's waiting arms. Tears spilled down their cheeks. "Mama!"

"Shh, you're safe now. It's all right." Emma held her close, buried her face in Babe's soft hair, and drank in her scent. "I'm here."

"That bad man tooked me, Mama. I woke up and he told me to stay quiet. I screamed and tried to bite him and he said he'd hurt you if I didn't do as he said." She reached up and caressed her mother's face, her expression full of fear at the memory. "I got quiet and he brought me here and tied me up. I told him I hated him and he stuffed his nasty handkerchief in my mouth."

Emma rocked her daughter as her tiny body shuddered with the force of her sobs. She found it odd that Babe didn't even recall Mack by name. A lot had happened since he'd been at their place, and Mack did look different with a beard and his loss of weight. It might be possible Babe really didn't recognize him. Tears ran down her own face as she imagined her daughter's terror, knowing she'd been helpless to rescue her at the time. "We're safe now. Josiah made everything safe."

Babe continued on as if Emma hadn't spoken. "I wiggled and wiggled until I got the hanky out of my mouth. I screamed as loud as I could, and my papa came to get me."

Emma looked around for Josiah and saw him standing nearby, tears streaming down his face as he wrestled with his own memories of the moment and his emotions. His jaw again clenched in anger.

After a moment, he cleared his throat. "He'd left her in the mine. It was dark inside there, and she was terrified." He looked away, clearly battling his desire to take Mack out for the pain he'd caused them.

"We're all safe now. Let it go, Josiah."

"I brought her back here, not knowing if you were dead or alive. I had to make a choice, and you said Babe came first. I'd been sneaking around to corner Mack from another direction when I heard Babe's faint cry. I secured her with Rocky and promised her I'd be back as soon as it was safe."

"God was watching out for her, Josiah. He used you to save her. I'll never be able to thank you enough."

He shook his head. "I had to leave you with a madman to find her. You'll never know the anguish that went through me knowing I had to make that choice. When I think of what could have happened. . ."

"But it didn't happen! You were able to find Babe and then come back to save me. You did it, Josiah. You kept us both safe, and in the process, you stopped Mack from hurting anyone else."

Josiah dropped to his knees and pulled both Emma and Babe into his arms.

Emma had never felt safer. "We're going to be all right, Josiah."

"Only if you promise never to leave my side," Josiah said, peering intently into her eyes. "I want you to marry me, and I want to be Papa to Babe. Please say yes."

Emma didn't take the time to answer. Her kiss said it all.

Babe interrupted, clapping her hands in glee. "I *told* you he would be my papa!"

Emma reluctantly pulled away from Josiah, and they both laughed. "That you did, Babe. That you did."

Josiah rose and tugged Emma to her feet, then picked up Babe, and in unspoken agreement they headed through the bushes toward Mack. Words tinged with guilt flowed from Josiah as they walked. "I lost control when his gun went off and I saw you fall. I hit him for all I was worth. I couldn't stop the blind rage I felt, knowing he'd almost succeeded in ruining me again. I realized the shot had gone high and that you were fine, but I pounded him anyway. I assured myself that you hadn't been shot, and then I ran to make sure Babe was still safe with Rocky."

"Thank you, Josiah. You did the right thing with Babe." She knew he'd feel guilt over his loss of restraint with Mack, but what man wouldn't have blown up at that point? "I love you."

Josiah stopped and pulled her into his arms again, holding her tightly against him. "I love you, too."

Mack was exactly as they'd left him, sagging against the tree.

Babe made a strangled sound at the sight, and Josiah

pulled her close against him, reassuring her that she was safe and that he'd not let Mack ever hurt her again. She melted into his arms and buried her face in his neck.

Mack glanced up at the trio, his face contorting into pain at the sight. "I'm so sorry. So very, very sorry." His eyes had cleared, and he seemed sober. "I need to explain."

Josiah motioned for him to continue.

"I know you trusted me like a brother, but you never knew my true thoughts. As the years passed, I grew to resent how naturally everything came to you and to Johnny. The women flocked to you each time we'd enter a new town, and you both seemed oblivious. I wanted that kind of attention from them, but you had it and didn't even care. You had a single focus—to earn your money and get your ranch."

Josiah interrupted. "Our ranch, Mack. You'd always been an equal partner, and I thought you knew that."

Mack shook his head. "I'd never be a part of what you two shared. I know you meant it when you said you'd cut me in, but I never broke through that bond the two of you had. I could never be as good as the two of you. You'd work hard and go to bed early. I never could settle down that way. I'd have to go out for a drink. . ."

"And we never judged you for it. It wasn't our place."

"No, but I judged myself. I knew I wasn't good enough to be a partner with you. I fought the urge to drink but always failed. I knew you had to be disappointed in me."

"Your guilt is your own, Mack. We prayed for you and loved you as a brother, nothing more, nothing less."

"I know. But one night—that last night—I decided I'd had enough. I wanted to see respect and pride in your eyes, not frustration and confusion when it came to me. I'd taken to gambling a bit, but that night things got out of hand. I couldn't seem to stop, so I went to the bank and ended up losing it all, our entire fortune. The one you'd cut me in on and we'd all worked hard for. We were so close to getting our ranch, and I was sure I could get that last bit of money and things would be great between us. But instead"—he shrugged—"I lost it all. Even what wasn't mine to lose. I couldn't face the two of you, so I skipped town. I figured I'd make the fortune somewhere else, and when I did, I'd return what I'd taken tenfold. Instead, I made my life more of a mess, ruined things for Emma, panicked, and here we all are." He looked at them all with pleading eyes. "I don't deserve your forgiveness, but I ask for it anyway. I want to make things right. I want to face up to what I've done."

Josiah measured him with his eyes but didn't say a word.

"Babe?" Mack's voice softened. "I'm so, so very sorry that I scared you. I'll never hurt you or scare you again. All right?"

Babe laid her head on Josiah's shoulder and stared at Mack for a few moments while they all waited. Finally, she raised her eyes to Josiah. "Mack's nice now?"

Josiah hesitated for a moment before answering. "It appears so."

Babe wiggled from his arms and stepped forward a few feet toward Mack. Her blond curls tumbled in disarray, making her appear younger than she was. "I forgive you. But stay nice now."

Emma thought her heart would break at her daughter's brave words. They could all take a lesson in forgiveness from her.

Mack nodded his agreement. "I'll stay nice, Babe."

They heard a rustling behind them. Help had finally arrived. Late, but at least they now had assistance. The sheriff and his men burst from the trees, surrounded Mack, untied him, and threw him on the ground.

Babe screamed, and Josiah dashed to grab her in his arms. She again buried her face in his neck, crying, "Papa, Papa."

Emma hurried forward to say that Mack had already been subdued. The sheriff handcuffed him and pulled him to his feet.

Josiah walked over and pulled Emma close.

"With all that's gone on, Josiah, what do you plan to do with Mack now?" She caressed his back then reached up to rub Babe's arm that stayed clenched around his neck.

Josiah stood silently, emotions warring on his features, before turning to face her. "Your love has shown me I can be redeemed and has given me a new hope. You've helped me find my way back to God, something I never thought I'd see happen. I'd pulled away too far. But you've shown me His love again and have allowed me to find love with you. With your agreement, I'd like to give the same chance to Mack." He paused. "He's a broken man, and I'd like to forgive him and help him find his way."

Emma threw her arms around him and pulled him close for a kiss. Josiah met her lips with his own.

Babe voiced her complaint at being squished between them, and Emma pulled slightly away, her laugh muffled against Josiah's shirt. "You're a good man, Josiah Andrews. I knew it from the start."

"Oh, the day you met me on your porch with a rifle pointed my way?"

"Well, maybe just after that." Emma felt her face flush at the memory. "More like when Babe threw herself into your arms and declared you her papa, and you stayed around anyway."

She looked up at the brave man who had done so much for her and Babe. His change of heart toward God was a joy to behold, and she relished watching him let go of his desire for revenge, opting instead for forgiveness.

Josiah's brown eyes searched hers. "You never gave me a formal answer to my question. Must you make me wait?"

"Question?" Emma was perplexed. He'd asked her many questions. She'd already shown her approval of his decision to forgive Mack.

"Babe, what are we gonna do with your mama?" Josiah's voice came across so tortured that even Babe had to giggle.

"He asked you to marry him, Mama. You didn't answer. You just kissed him. Say yes! Please!" Babe tilted her blond head and smiled in an endearing plea. Josiah had to adjust his grip to prevent her from tumbling out of his arms.

"Yes, say yes, please?" Josiah echoed, his grin just as irresistible. He had a wild look about him, dirt smudged across his face from his tumble with Mack, dark hair blowing around his shoulders, and his dark brown eyes sparkling with mischief. He looked more like a savage outlaw than a civilized lawman. "Let me be your husband and be a proper papa to this little girl here."

"I thought my kiss said yes for me," Emma hedged, shrieking as Josiah used the arm that held her close to tickle her with no mercy. "All right, yes, I'll marry you!"

Cheers broke loose behind them, and Emma turned mortified eyes to the sheriff and his men.

" 'Bout time you tied the knot again, Emma," one called out.

"Yes, we thought you were gonna let this perfect papa for Babe get away," another added. "We even had a small bet going. . ." He glanced quickly over at the sheriff. "Er. . . uh. . .I mean, we all had an opinion on how things would turn out."

Sheriff Bates shook his head and brought Mack over to where the happy couple stood. "Best wishes to you both. Why don't you all get squared away, then come by my office in the morning. Until then, we'll make sure Mack has everything he needs, and you can decide how you want to handle things at that time."

"I appreciate it, Sheriff. We'll see you in the mornin', then."

Emma watched as Josiah and Mack exchanged glances, and her heart melted at the peace that filled Mack's face as he took in the forgiveness in Josiah's.

Josiah led them back to Rocky, where the horse now stood in wait. He set Babe gently on the ground and walked over to dig around in his saddlebags. "I had a special surprise to give my little girl, but I seem to have misplaced it."

Babe frowned and moved closer. Emma held her back, catching Josiah's eye and noting the twinkle in it.

"What was it, Papa?"

"Well, give me a minute. I'm sure it's here somewhere." He fumbled around a bit more, though there was no way the object he sought could be lost in the bag. "Ah, here it is!" He turned with an exuberant grin, hiding the item behind his back.

Babe literally jumped with excitement. "What is it?

Show me! Please!" The latter comment was added only after Emma's nudge to her back.

Josiah dropped to his knee and pulled a brown package from behind him with a flourish. Babe pouted her dismay as the surprise still lay hidden.

He held it out, and Babe glanced up at Emma. Emma nodded, and Babe tenderly peeled back the wrapper.

Even Emma gasped at the beauty of the exquisite porcelain doll that lay before them. "Oh, Josiah. . ."

Babe squealed with glee as Josiah handed her the doll and then carefully swung his daughter-to-be through the air with his strong arms. Babe cradled the doll in her arms and looked at Josiah with pure adoration.

Emma blinked back tears of joy. A papa to swing her daughter into the air, just like in Babe's dreams. And even more important, a man to share Emma's life, one who would also cherish her greatest treasure.

Emma watched her daughter's dream unfold at the same time her heart's desire for a loving husband was met.

epilogue

Emma stood before the large looking glass and studied her appearance. Her face glowed in the mirror's reflection. Her eyes were bright with joy. It was hard to believe the happy bride who peered back was her. She brought her hands up to her face, trying to cool her hot cheeks.

Katie and Liza stood beside her.

"Stop fretting," Katie admonished. "You'll splotch your cheeks."

"I'm not fretting. I'm trying to see if this is real or a dream."

"It's no dream, dear. Your handsome prince awaits you on the other side of that door."

"Oh my." Emma dropped to sit in a nearby chair. "What am I doing? I'm really marrying him. I hardly know him! Is this the right thing for Babe? For me? Help!" It was a fake plea. She knew Josiah was the man for her.

Both women laughed.

Katie placed her hands firmly on Emma's shoulders. "Josiah is the best thing to happen to both of you in a long, long time. He's smitten, not only by you, but by your daughter, as well. I think if you refused to marry him at this point, she'd go ahead and make him her papa without you. You no longer have a choice."

Emma grinned. Her friend was right. Babe had known the man would be her papa from the moment he rode into their yard. Emma was the one who took some time, though in her heart she'd known he was special at that first glimpse, too.

Liza pulled her to her feet. "We need to stuff you into some more layers. Your groom won't want to wait forever."

"That's such a flattering thought. Thank you." Emma turned sideways and perused her side profile. Whew, as slender as ever.

"My comment didn't refer to your size. I merely stated that we need more than petticoats on you before you make your appearance."

Katie lifted the gorgeous wedding gown, and Liza took the other side. They raised it over Emma's head and carefully lowered it over her finished hair. The two women had worked her long tresses into a vision of beauty. Her hair was upswept from her neck, and tendrils of curls hung loosely to frame her face, just the way Josiah liked it.

"Mama, I'm a fairy princess," Babe called from across the room.

Liza had created both of their dresses. While Emma's was an elegant work that hugged close to her body before gradually widening at the hem where it touched the floor, Babe's was a concoction of pink and white. She now twirled about the room so quickly that Emma was afraid the little girl would fall and hit her head or get sick.

"Slow down, baby doll. You don't want to miss the ceremony. Your new papa will be sad if you can't make our family day."

Babe froze and swayed as her eyes struggled with the sudden loss of motion. She plopped down on her bottom and balanced herself with a hand on each side of her legs.

"I don't want to make my papa sad."

The ladies behind her muttered and tugged as they forced the multitude of tiny buttons at the back of her dress to close.

Babe rose slowly to her feet. She smoothed the dress. "Is it okay?"

"Your dress is fine, and you look gorgeous." The dress had puffy white sleeves and a high waist, pulled in with a shiny pink sash. The full skirt featured layers of white and pink, so when Babe spun, the different colors parted like the petals of a flower. The effect was stunning, and Babe couldn't resist spinning in circles to watch it flow.

Emma felt so proud of her friend's skill and the intricacy of her work. Liza now had more work than she could handle, and women were lining up to get her to make their next dresses for each and every occasion. She knew Liza and Petey were going to be fine.

Katie had fixed Babe's hair in a miniature version of Emma's own. She looked precious.

"There," Katie said to Emma. "I think we have it. Step back and let us look at you."

Emma did as she was told.

The women stared at her until she felt like a horse on the auction block. "Well?"

"You're breathtaking."

"Josiah's going down in a dead faint when he sees you."

"Mama, you look like a princess, too!"

Strangely enough, the odd conglomeration of comments calmed her pounding heart. "Thank you. I think I'm ready to marry my future husband now." As a matter of fact, she couldn't become Mrs. Josiah Andrews a moment too soon.

Her heart fully embraced the idea. He completed her in a way she'd not realized since losing Matthew.

Instead of feeling sad at the thought of her late husband, she felt peace. She knew Matthew would be happy that she'd married again and had found someone to love her and Babe. She also knew he'd be relieved to know Babe had a papa looking out for her. As stunning as the young child was, Josiah would have his hands full chasing off suitors before they knew it. Already he complained about the "attentions" of Jimmy and Petey.

The door banged open against the wall as Petey burst through. "Mother! They're ready for you. Hurry!"

Liza laughed and took her son's hand and steered him back out the door.

Katie took both of Emma's hands in her own. "Are you okay? I can wait and walk with you if you need me to."

Emma leaned over to kiss her dear friend's cheek. "I'm finer than I've been in a long, long time. Thanks for caring."

"I'll always care, and I'm always here for you. I'm happy you've found Josiah. He's a great man."

Katie left and closed the door behind her.

"Well, Babe, this is it."

"You mean we're *finally* going to marry Josiah, Mama?"

Emma laughed. "Yes, we're finally going to marry Josiah."

Babe dropped her voice to a whisper. "Thanks for saying yes."

"You're welcome," Emma whispered back. She reached for her daughter's hand and clasped it in her own. "Let's go get our man."

Mack waited for them on the porch. "You look a vision. Both of you."

"Thank you, Mack. That means a lot." Emma was thrilled that he'd made a full turnabout in personality and now worked to make amends with Josiah. She quietly thanked God for the progress he'd made.

"I mean it. Your example of forgiveness and love, not to mention lack of concern about riches, made me realize there was more to life than I'd realized. I thought money brought happiness. Then I found out it caused grief like I'd never known before. I lost the two most important things in my life—Josiah and Johnny." He paused. "I can't get Johnny back, but I can work to make things right with Josiah."

"You know money isn't important to Josiah, either. You can't pay him back financially."

"I know. But if I can get my life right with my Lord, I think that will please your husband and my best friend. What do you think?"

"I think you'd do him proud if you follow through on that plan."

Mack moved forward and crooked his arm. "Now, let's get going and marry you off to that man before he—or your bouncing daughter over there—passes out from the pressure."

Emma called for Babe, and the little girl ran over to stare up at Mack. He offered her his other arm, and Emma held her breath in anticipation. Mack had come a long way, but would he suffer a setback if Babe rejected him again?

She needn't have worried. Babe sent Mack her most charming grin and happily attempted to copy her mother's hold on his arm. "Take us to our wedding, Mr. Mack. Please."

"Don't mind if I do," Mack spouted back playfully. "Oh, wait. I have something for both of you." He dug a small bag out of his pocket and withdrew two delicate necklaces. Each held a small nugget of gold. "These are for you both, matching necklaces that I had made from the first nuggets I ever pulled from the claim."

Emma reached for hers while Mack bent down to fasten the other around Babe's neck. "It's perfect! Oh, Mack, we gave you these nuggets for you to keep. You shouldn't have done this."

"I did, and I wanted to. The gold belongs to you, and I want you to see that I'm giving back the firstfruits of my labor. I wanted to give you a gift, and this felt like the right one to give."

"We'll both treasure the necklaces, won't we, baby doll?"

Babe still stood in awe at wearing her first piece of jewelry ever. "Yes, ma'am, we will."

Mack looked embarrassed at their appreciation and urged them on to meet Josiah. But a happy grin filled his face as they went.

The trio walked around the corner of the house into the crowded side yard. The flowers had burst into bloom the day before, as if wanting to add their beauty to the celebration of love.

Josiah stood next to the pastor, and his face filled with such adoration as their eyes met that Emma began to cry. He took a step forward as she watched, and the pastor put an arm out to stop him from moving up the aisle to his bride.

"Now don't shed too many tears and miss seeing your own wedding, Emma." Mack's whisper brought her to her senses.

She was on her way to her new life with the man of her dreams, with Babe by her side. There was no way she'd blur that vision with tears. She held her head high and moved forward to meet the man she loved.

A Letter To Our Readers

Dear Reader:

In order that we might better contribute to your reading enjoyment, we would appreciate your taking a few minutes to respond to the following questions. We welcome your comments and read each form and letter we receive. When completed, please return to the following:

Fiction Editor
Heartsong Presents
PO Box 719
Uhrichsville, Ohio 44683

1. Did you enjoy reading *Treasure in the Hills* by Paige Winship Dooly?
   ❑ Very much! I would like to see more books by this author!
   ❑ Moderately. I would have enjoyed it more if

   _____

   _____

   _____

2. Are you a member of **Heartsong Presents**? ❑ Yes ❑ No
   If no, where did you purchase this book? _____

   _____

3. How would you rate, on a scale from 1 (poor) to 5 (superior), the cover design? _____

4. On a scale from 1 (poor) to 10 (superior), please rate the following elements.

   _____ Heroine   _____ Plot
   _____ Hero   _____ Inspirational theme
   _____ Setting   _____ Secondary characters

5. These characters were special because? _____

_____

_____

6. How has this book inspired your life? _____

_____

_____

7. What settings would you like to see covered in future
   Heartsong Presents books? _____

_____

_____

8. What are some inspirational themes you would like to see
   treated in future books? _____

_____

_____

9. Would you be interested in reading other **Heartsong
   Presents** titles? ❑ Yes ❑ No

10. Please check your age range:
    ❑ Under 18   ❑ 18-24
    ❑ 25-34   ❑ 35-45
    ❑ 46-55   ❑ Over 55

Name _____

Occupation _____

Address _____

City, State, Zip_____

Presents

HEARTSONG PRESENTS

If you love Christian romance...

$10.⁹⁹

You'll love Heartsong Presents' inspiring and faith-filled romances by today's very best Christian authors. . .Wanda E. Brunstetter, Mary Connealy, Susan Page Davis, Cathy Marie Hake, and Joyce Livingston, to mention a few!

When you join Heartsong Presents, you'll enjoy four brand-new, mass market, 176-page books—two contemporary and two historical—that will build you up in your faith when you discover God's role in every relationship you read about!

Mass Market 176 Pages

Imagine. . .four new romances every four weeks—with men and women like you who long to meet the one God has chosen as the love of their lives...all for the low price of $10.99 postpaid.

To join, simply visit www.heartsong presents.com or complete the coupon below and mail it to the address provided.

YES! Sign me up for Heartsong!

NEW MEMBERSHIPS WILL BE SHIPPED IMMEDIATELY!
Send no money now. We'll bill you only $10.99 postpaid with your first shipment of four books. Or for faster action, call 1-740-922-7280.

NAME _____

ADDRESS_____

CITY_____ STATE _____ ZIP _____

MAIL TO: HEARTSONG PRESENTS, P.O. Box 721, Uhrichsville, Ohio 44683
or sign up at WWW.HEARTSONGPRESENTS.COM